W9-AYQ-525

"Skittering on the edge of total farce, Miller succeeds in being both comic and touching. His zany characters are made to bear a shadow likeness to much that is recognizable in the U.S. today—a young nation's yearning for swift solutions, the hope of impossible perfection, the lingering evangelical zeal of frontier religion, the fear that a great human dream has been laid waste in the pillaging of a rich continent for material well-being. With much skill and a kind of love Miller shows these crackpots are our own."

—LIFE

"Ribald and raucous comedy . . . the most unsparing essay on the American cultural landscape since Humbert Humbert went his desperate motel hegira across the continent."

—THE NATION

Other Crest Books by Warren Miller

THE WAY WE LIVE NOW

THE COOL WORLD

90 MILES FROM HOME

FLUSH TIMES

The Crest imprint on outstanding books is your guarantee of informative and entertaining reading

WARREN MILLER

looking for the general

A Crest Reprint
FAWCETT PUBLICATIONS, INC., GREENWICH, CONNECTICUT
MEMBER OF AMERICAN BOOK PUBLISHERS COUNCIL, INC.

THE AUTHOR WISHES TO THANK
THE ACADEMY AND NATIONAL INSTITUTE
OF ARTS AND LETTERS
FOR A GRANT WHICH AIDED
IN THE WRITING OF THIS NOVEL.

A Crest Book published by arrangement with
McGraw-Hill Book Company, Inc.

Copyright © 1964 by Warren Miller
All rights reserved, including the right to
reproduce this book or portions thereof.

Library of Congress Catalog Card Number: 63-21785

First Crest printing, March 1965

Crest Books are published by Fawcett World Library,
67 West 44th Street, New York, N. Y. 10036.
Printed in the United States of America.

Earth, you darling, I will!

RILKE

. . . I am fully aware of the risk I am taking in proposing to communicate my views concerning contemporary events. . . . I refer to those reports reaching us from all corners of the earth, rumors of round objects that flash through the troposphere and stratosphere, and go by the name of Flying Saucers. . . . These rumors, or the possible physical existence of such objects, seem to me so significant that I feel myself compelled, as once before when events were brewing of fateful consequence for Europe, to sound a note of warning. . . . It is not presumption that drives me, but my conscience as a psychiatrist that bids me fulfill my duty and prepare those few who will hear me for coming events which are in accord with the end of an era. . . . We are now nearing that great change which may be expected when the spring-point enters Aquarius.

CARL JUNG, *Flying Saucers*

Oh! what a desire I have, cried the Marchioness, *that there might happen some great shipwreck, which would scatter here a great number of these people, then we might consider at ease their extraordinary figures. But,* replied I, *if they should be able to swim on the exterior surface of our air, and from thence to a curiosity to see us, should fish for us as we do for fishes, would this please you? Why not?* answered she, *laughing. As for me I would readily throw myself into their nets, only to have the pleasure of seeing those who fished for me.*

FONTENELLE,
Conversations upon the Plurality of Worlds

To Ned Curley

A Note to the Reader: The author does not wish to be credited with too much imagination and must, therefore, point out that nearly all the ideas expressed by the characters in this book are to be found in certain magazines and books published in this country, and that these ideas are shared by a small army of our countrymen.

Although the act of sabotage described in this novel is based on an actual event that occurred in the American West two years ago, all the characters are, of course fictional.

one

WHAT GOOD luck not to have fallen into their hands! I've escaped their brutal shock machines, what *they* call therapy. Memory is therefore inviolate, untouched; as it should be: such a precious little thing, that membrane on which now so much is written—and in what fantastic symbols, calligraphic scratches, pictograms, ideoforms—that must be transcribed. I have fed so much knowledge into this machine, a fantastically complex programming. How terrible if now it begin to stutter and produce mere gibberish; or, worse, halt in the middle and refuse to go on, keeping all of this for itself as nourishment. They have minds of their own, you know.

Electrodes would have destroyed it all. But it's a chancy business either way, isn't it? Cure (by what odd logic, I wonder) is destruction; all would be lost. That barbarous machine, an alchemist run amuck, converts pure gold to a chaos of dust. Memory then no more than a million motes sparkling a little when touched by sun, revealing—oh how slyly!—its source in gold, perhaps in sun itself.

How knowledgeable the mad have become. Have you noticed this in your friends? Yes, I prefer the word *mad*; I do. It is exact and forthright, has not the dreadful gentility of *nervous breakdown*: something so spinsterish about that term, redolent of dresser drawers that are far too neat. But certain items never washed? found rolled up in corners? I think so, I think so; there is a sour odor about it, a smell of installment buying, small bank loans, electrical appliances. No, I prefer to say that I was touched by the wing of madness, in Pittsburgh, at the lab, while working on the problem of the thermal thicket.

two

AT THE LAB now (then) we have no lack of resources, latest equipment, computers big as blockhouses, assistants without number. It was not always so, but now it is under contract to the Air Force. We produce the findings they ask for. This makes for tensions. (I am oversimplifying, of course; there is more to it than this. There is science itself.) My colleague Wilson has responded to the situation by falling victim to terrible headaches. Several days every month he stays home in a darkened room. His wife's solicitude has made him tyrannical. How ugly men become who have *married well*: one has only to look at them to see that their every wish is gratified, immediately and without question, no matter how perverse. They become flaccid and wear, soon enough, the white face of the pimp. Tyrants are the most domesticated of animals; outside their pens, like pigs, they are lost.

Wilson was not always so. In England, during the war, when we were radar technicians, he had a poacher's leanness and a poacher's health. Then there was no one to do everything for him and he went after the factory girls and the hard-handed muscular women of the Land Army (oh their bearish embraces, the weathered skin!) and took them in fields, doorways, phone booths, wherever he could. We all did. How delicious fatigue was then—only the young can know: to lie down between the coarse sheets of an army cot at three in the morning and *listen* to the fatigue in one's bones ticking like a clock; and wake at seven, ready for more, the tiredness unwound like a watchspring. To go into the town again, wander past monuments to the fish-and-chips queue (remember?), the girls like cards in a file drawer, waiting to be riffled or flicked over, carefully, one by one until—*there!*

Wilson then is not Wilson now. Neither am I. Now we calculate, make demands, have lost all recklessness and the joy of being indiscriminate; we think of marrying well and of second cars. We have forgot everything. Wilson certainly has. Youth has ticked away like the old fatigue but has not left us refreshed and ready for more. We are ready for nothing now; or, actually, in our desperation, we are ready for anything. Ready in this sense: that we are always waiting. (Haven't you felt it? Surely you have; you must: don't you, for weeks and months at a time, expect at any moment your name will be called out and someone will hand you a prize?)

So then, Wilson has his headaches and I broke in two. Result: a lateral turbulence, as we physicists say. It is a phenomenon well known to astronomers; mechanically speaking, a form of disorder. Nebulae especially are susceptible to it. Call it a will to die. It is inherent in all things. Even atoms decay, the law tells us, every five billion years. Or to live forever? Yes, certainly, that too. It is all part of the same thing. Even the general knows this. The general knows very little, but he knows this.

But here is the question: is disorder reversible? The second of law of thermodynamics declares it is not: disordered motion can never completely be converted into ordered motion. It is a hard law, I grant; and we were not even consulted. But face up to it, friend: where mathematics begins, there democracy ends.

three

THE GENERAL called me in to his office that day, the morning of the night I dreamed of the thermal thicket. Nothing odd about that; we often dream the solutions to problems that wrack us by day (and, obviously, by night). In my dream I saw it as a churning, twisting band, a thick bowstring of turbulence consisting of brambles, shards, bobby pins, barbed wire, tacks, spiny thorns, bedsprings. How to get the rockets safely through: that is the problem. Something (let me attempt to make this readily understandable for you)—something like the sound barrier, if you will, but infinitely (that word!) more complicated. The solution came to me in dream, jolted me awake with its elegant simplicity: A counterforce! I had it: the idea of counterforce: to destroy that fantastic heat with heat even more intense. Oh yes, laughable now, of course; but then, in that green dawn light, how I was seized by the idea, that vision of release.

In the morning, at the lab, I walked down the long cinder-block (nothing is really finished) corridor to my office, holding this idea before me. It glittered in that gloom, was protected by an aura as in a Sunday-school print of a holy object. Exultant, for I had grasped it at last, I wanted to run; but the security officer, Jerome Walz, was prowling his beat. He smiled when he recognized me and nodded several times; as he passed he whispered in execrable American-Polish: "Yock she mosh, kid?" Letting me know that he knew, wanting me to know he knew. They are sly; they forget nothing; they have a rodent cunning.

Without turning round I stopped and cursed him—Walz! Walz! Walz!—seeing my idea crumble, collapse, fall to the floor, its aura dry up and disappear like angel hair or ectoplasm.

"Come in, Bill!" the general cried; but it was only the show of camaraderie and good-fellowship; it lacked the old fervor, only the form remained; like the sign above his head, which had begun to yellow at its edges: *Those Who Have the WILL TO LOSE Are Not Wanted in This Shop!* The operation he had permitted them to perform had aged him; he has a little melon of a belly now and as it cxpands his face grows smaller; it's as if the body were feeding off the head.

In England, during the war, he was commander of the base where Wilson and I were stationed, two technical sergeants among many; but seven years later, when I came to the lab looking for a job, doctorate in hand, he remembered my name (the old one)—sure sign of a great administrator. He had resigned from the Air Force to become administrative director of the laboratory; and the contract followed him, a profitable vapor trail the board duly admired. His reward, one heard, was a bonus both handsome and tax-free (Wilson's idea of heaven).

"Sit down, Bill," the general said. "I want your opinion on this." He held up the familiar blue folder that Research Department always wraps around its reports to give a spurious air of permanence to their findings. "A little problem I set them working on some months ago, Bill. Read it when you have a moment and let me know your thinking. Tomorrow? Can you? I don't want to lose any time on this. I haven't got it any more, Bill."

I was about to utter some soothing words at this point, but the general added: "None of us has the time any more, Bill."

He took back the report and called in Greystone, who had been sergeant-major at the base in England. He still looked uncomfortable in civvies, and always appeared to be embarrassed at being seen in them. Too old and too shy for masquerades, that was Greystone. Like me, still unmarried; but he gave no indication that he was haunted by a sense of failure. Well, he has little learning; he is a superior file clerk, nothing more. (Here is evidence of my honesty, friend. How easy it would be, after the fact, to boast and claim that in Greystone I had always sensed something hidden, a mysterious force under that bland mask he wore. But I did not, and will not say I did.)

The general handed him the report. He said, "Greystone, stamp this Urgent."

"We have no Urgent stamp, sir."

"We haven't?"

"Secret, Top Secret, and Most Confidential, sir, are all we have. We used to have For Your Eyes Only, but Security took it away from us."

"I wonder why?" the general said, and Greystone and I joined him in the silence that followed this question. "All right, that will be all, Greystone." He gave me back the blue folder. "Take it as it is, Bill, but in your mind's eye see the word *Urgent* stamped on it, will you, Bill?"

All I saw in my mind's eye as I walked out of the office was the general's head, melting away like wax; I saw it shrink to the size of a button. Passing Greystone's desk in the outer office, where he sat with his back to a great wall map of America—how dark he is, how impassive his face; like a stone idol squatting at the general's door, he guards him against infidels—I nodded, and he looked up and snapped back his head, his way of throwing into place a strand of black hair that always detached itself and fell across his forehead.

"How's it going, Brown?" he said.

"Fine. But . . ."

He smiled. "Security bugging you?" He raised his eyebrows, a mannerism he had picked up from the chief. He lowered his voice. "Don't let on I told you, Bill, but they are even keeping an eye on the general." He nodded toward the report I held in my hand. "I'll be real interested to hear what you think of that, Bill."

I looked at the title now for the first time: *Matter, Organic, from Outer Space. An Inquiry.*

I returned to my office and lay down on the couch; I am always tired now: it has no savor; it does not tick.

four

DRIVING THROUGH urban decay that was once suburbia (we'll lick this problem yet, ho ho), I often think: this limestone earth did not exist a billion years ago. And looking up, I think: nor stars or the sun nine billion years before that. Oh Pittsburghers, if you knew it, if you knew! Think if the whole town knew: the fright, the fear, thousands scrabbling to seek a handhold on pavements, lampposts; all suddenly stricken with the worst disease of man: the terrible vertigo that the notion of infinity and nothingness always brings with it; and its echoes, echoes more terrible than the sound that brought them forth—of a world of eternal duration, of a world that arose in continuity out of nothing.

What if we told them all we know? Someday, of course, when the sheer weight and overwhelmingly horrifying bulk of our knowledge become more than we can bear—then, well then, of course we'll tell.

What we ought to do is release it a little at a time, hopefully, like poison to snake charmers; once a month, perhaps, issue a proclamation. The

first proclamation

¶ Pittsburghers: All matters existing in the universe today once existed compressed into a narrow space.

That would be enough for the first; then, allow them a month to live with their imaginings and learn to *see* the hideous meaning of it, of that explosion, so awful, so frightful in its immense daring, its enormous celestial bravado. Out of dust, out of gas, out of (probably) a hydrogen atom we came; for ancestor: a molecule with a fluke, a sport of nature, a *joke!* Now a man, living in the middle of (geologically speaking, an Ice Age; and still, after five billion years, lacking the sense to go out in the rain and make our escape from ignorance to knowledge. We must know, we must know: They must come and tell us who know so much more. And They will come—oh if I did not believe that!—They will come and They will tell us; out of inarticulated time They will come and They will tell us. (As a matter of fact, I've known this for quite some time: since the war, when we saw the evidence of it on the radar screens.)

I lay on the couch in my office, the blue report on my chest—not forgotten, but I knew it all already—and thought about these things. There was a mouse in the wastebasket, but the phone did not ring nor did Wilson come bursting through the connecting door from his office. He had been home, sick, for several days now—almost a week. I had forgot to phone his wife and ask how he was feeling. They would be hurt. I decided to stop and see them, that afternoon, on my way home. They adore having witnesses to their happiness.

Leaving at 4:30—at four there had come a memo from the general: *Have you read it yet, Bill?,* which I ignored—I brazened past the pickets who, in a tight circle, kept a permanent vigil at our main doors. (Wilson leaves by the back, parks his car across the street.) The usual signs: Don't Kill Our Children, etc. Today there were also Quakers, who maintain a silent vigil. They just stand there. They are so much more effective than the others: those plain people have a dramatic sense that the more flamboyant will never understand. As I crossed the picket line, the Quakers looked at me with incomprehension and love; I hated them and closed my eyes. Getting into my car, I looked back at the building—why? what made me do it?—and saw: Jerome Walz, just inside the glass doors, watching. He smiled; then spoke—I could read his lips: *Yock she mosh.*

five

WHEELING THROUGH suburbs layered like geologic strata, having passed post-World War I and entered pre-Depression, a stone's throw now from post-World War II (do they think of themselves as survivors?), going downhill fast to post-Korea; heading toward rolling country now where nestle housing development pre-Southeast Asia, where the Wilsons live, all unaware, in its menacing comfort. (We all know, surely, that there will be no post-Southeast Asia?) (No; in fact, we do not all know. The Wilsons, for example, do not know.)

Leaving post-Korea—the green wood warped, of course, and revealing the lathe bones, like a rib cage—windows stuck, doors slightly askew in their frames; can all be seen by a trained eye (try it); requires, already, regular monthly visits by licensed exterminators. And because the roof leaks, Mother remembers when she was a girl—it is her only tie with the past—and reads the stains on the bedroom ceiling: sepia polyps, islands of Madagascar, east coast of Africa, the profile of Mr. George Benway (father of her best friend in 1936). Don't laugh; even such roots are better than none at all; but let us be strictly truthful: none is worth a damn.

Leaving then, as I said, post-Korea, I issued Proclamation Number 2. It dealt with the spaces between stars. Hideous. It had to be withdrawn; I shouted myself down like a poll-tax senator: Will you yield, sir! I yielded; withdrew it. Too early to issue it; they are not ready. They may never be ready, our people, because they have forgot too much. (In the Second Proclamation I had used the example of the imaginary miniature model of the universe, the earth having a diameter of .0000003937 of an inch—an invisible speck, mind you—and the sun with a diameter of .00003937; the distance between the two being, of course, .003937. In this microscopic model of *our* universe [ho ho] the star nearest to the sun would have to be placed 165 feet [approx.] away; while the Milky Way—still keeping to this scale, mind you—would have to be 620 miles wide, 930 miles deep. Think about that, friend; think about that a little.)

Yes, we have forgot too much. It was not always so. Why was it, do you think, the Indians ran with such eagerness and joy to welcome the Spanish savages and call them gods? What thrilling urgency was in them, seeing the ships, white sails, anchor-splash in the bright blue waters, to run knee-deep into the shallows, so eager to call those West European peasants gods and themselves slaves? What? Surely it was that, unlike us, they had not forgot; the Indians had not forgot and they mistook those men—swineherds! failed second sons!—for gods and ancestors, for that ideal, idyllic race that fled this earth when Atlantis was destroyed.

six

BEATRICE WILSON came to the door, the door on the upper part of the split-level pre-Southeast Asia home they occupied, those two: eight rooms, garage, carport and, of course, barbecue pit. One of their neighbors (he was said to be melancholic) had recently immolated himself in his great two-family pit; his charred body was found with two dead chickens and a bowl of barbecue sauce at his side; it caused a great but short-lived scandal. The Wilsons lived in this house, paid for it by the month, and being emancipated and superior people, made fun of it, pretended to loathe it.

"B-Bill, how are you?" she said.

"Why is everyone asking me how I am?" I said, and followed her into the upper-level living room: one side of it was two stories high, then it fell away to a wall of ordinary height; this was because of the pitched roof. It gave the impression that the builder, in his haste, had forgot something vital. He must be forgiven; the poor man is working under the pressure of memory. He remembers '41 when the supplies ran out and his houses were left unfinished till that war was over. He does not know he's living in the middle of the Ice Age; but he knows other things and he knows he's got to hurry. Southeast Asia hanging over his head. When will it go?

When will it go? Bullying his workers, the question haunts him; and seeing the living room with its queer ceiling he throws up his hands and says What the hell, let it go, we got no time to fix it. He is thinking of Southeast Asia; knows that wars in the tropics last a long time (enforced idleness of troops during rainy season, lack of roads, etc.). He'll never get the copper pipes for the plumbing then; he'll wait forever for iron rods and watch his workers walk off the job to join up, QM and Seabees. Who, these days, has not got a nightmare of his own?

Beatrice settled herself, her flowing skirt and oversize sweater, in a foam rubber chair. She is a tall, well-built woman and her clothes are always at least one size too big for her; she wants to give the impression she's wasting away, that under the bulk of sweater and skirt there moves a girlish body, a sylph. Hips give her away. Alas. It is the mark of the well-married. Like her clothes, she wears her hair too big for her head; it is wound loosely and sits there, not really a part of her, like a queen mother's hat or the kind of nest long-legged birds build who have difficulty flying. She is thirty-five, a monument to the failure of progressive education, whose product she is.

She wore pearls. She touched them; she was always, apparently, wondering were they really there. Like most women of her kind, and for all her seeming contemporaneity, she would have been far happier at the turn of the century, as a member, perhaps, of some Pre-Raphaelite group, married to a second-rate painter who designs wallpapers on Sundays and does her portrait whenever he feels the Inspiration. For some reason I always *see* Beatrice surrounded with those evil-looking lilies the Pre-Raphaelites so adored. Symbols of adultery, surely? Always open, long-stemmed, bending; their designs are curiously full of mouths and orifices. And it is well known that the Rossettis seldom took baths; although, of course, hardly ever mentioned.

"I came to see George," I said. "How is he?"

"Then you don't know? He did not tell you?"

This is Beatrice's idea of drawing-room talk. "Evidently not," I said I'd rather cut off my right arm than encourage her.

"But he told me he was going to tell you. I was wondering why you had not come by, Billy."

"Tell me what?"

"He went to Nevada to give up smoking."

"To Nevada? There is some famous *kur* in Nevada, Beatrice?"

"We have that cabin, you know, near Lake Tahoe, and . . ."

"As a matter of fact, Beatrice, I do *not* know that you have a cabin near Lake Tahoe."

She adjusted her skirt again and felt for her pearls; I could have told her they were still there. "I was sure we had told you about that cabin. It is a very little cabin, Billy. We bought it last summer. George wants to retire there."

"I see."

"I know what you're thinking, Billy, and I call it unfair."

I was sure she did. I had once gone on at some length, over coffee with Beatrice and George, about those young couples of our generation who, within two years after the birth of what they *know* will be the last child, rush out to buy a cemetery plot and begin to count the days until retirement, to count stock options, to count the money in retirement funds, to count social security benefits. And if they knew—oh if they knew—the date of their death, how they would count the days; and if that date could be bought, they'd buy it. But we aren't yet quite rich enough for that; soon, though, soon we will be. We will choose it ourselves—imagine it!—like selecting a diamond or furs, we'll just walk into the elegant shop and say, *That one! I want that one!* (We're a lucky people.)

How we careen toward the safety of old age; Sunday drivers, yes, but so well covered it is almost more profitable to crash than not, eh, friend?

"We aren't like that," Beatrice said. "I assure you, Billy"—and here she paused to laugh—"I assure you we haven't been out buying cemetery plots."

"You don't have to go out to do it any more. Salesmen come to the door now with prospectuses, photos, folding maps." One had knocked on my door only the week before, mouth full of a set speech on the pleasures of *passing on,* but only *if* you are prepared. (I spotted him at once, of course: he was from Intelligence;

around his eyes and mouth were those give-away lines of anxiety and desperation.)

"We'd be the very last to do such a thing," she said, giving it all away, crossing her legs. "No, George just wanted to get away from all temptation, to be far from tobacconists and the pressures that drive him to cigarettes. He was up to three packs a day, you know."

"I suppose," I said, "I suppose it was that report on smoking and lung cancer that caused him to rush off to Tahoe?" Incredible; surrounded by evidence that denies it definitively they persist in believing it is cigarettes cause cancer.

She looked at her knees. "Actually, Bill"—and now her voice became unusually husky, indicating she was plumbing depths of consciousness even she had been unaware of—"actually, I don't think it was the report, or the idea of cancer, *or* the fear of death—"

"George has always been something of a faddist. As his oldest friend, I think I have the right to say this."

"—although that is not to deny (and of course you have the right to say it, Bill) that unconsciously all these things may have been operating; but it is more than that. Actually, Bill, I think it's that George wants to change his life."

"I see." Common complaint; poor George.

"And he saw those three packs a day as the clearest, most readily available symbol of his old life. That is what I think, Bill." She folded her hands now and rested them on her knee; her father had been a judge and she had picked up all sorts of nasty judicial habits from him: for example, she sometimes *cleared her throat* before speaking.

I thought about George, alone at Tahoe, with his complaint, his habit, and his wish. How typical of him to hit on such a superficial symbol of our atrophied lives, those innocent, nicely designed cigarette packs. I did not speak of this to Beatrice, of course; but could think of nothing else to say (it was one of those moments) and Beatrice's eyes went soft and I expected her to lean forward and say, "I'll just run up and put on something more comfortable, you wait here." Tall women have a potential for a coy vulgarity that is astonishing. Whenever we were alone for any length of time I sensed in her a *readiness*, a very subtle (but marked) forward lean; it required some presence on my part to pretend to ignore it. Once, on just such an occasion, she had said to me, "Bachelors, of a certain age, are so terribly mysterious. Do you know that, Billy?" Another time, before that, at dinner, she had said, "George, if anything ever happens to you, you know that I shall turn to Bill." George was embarrassed for her, of course, but he carried it off rather well, saluted me and said, "Good luck!" While I bowed to Beatrice and said, "At your service." Ugly.

And yet, subtly, in a curious way, this ridiculous exchange created a bond that, for a moment, held us unmoving, unmovable. (That was the night, over coffee, I had suspected them of buying a burial plot.)

Lurking just below the sophisticated (ho ho) surface of every Radcliffe girl is the innocent vulgarity of a coal-town waitress, the kind who belch and then, quite seriously, say, "It must have been something I ate." That is why I always expected Beatrice to say something like "I'll just run up and put on something more comfortable" or, worse, "Mustn't touch!" One or the other; perhaps both. Most likely both: she has a remarkable talent for taking as she gives; something learned, no doubt, at her mother's knee, a woman who still wears her husband's fraternity pin.

Silence burgeoned and the slanty ceiling oppressed me; I half expected that at any moment it would snap closed, pinning us together between wall and ceiling in the builder's elementary trap: two hearts beating there à la Poe, ho ho. Meanwhile (I believe) Beatrice toyed with the notion of adultery. Was that also part of the builder's elementary trap, or just the suburban triumph over mercy and justice, or simply the pre-Asian funk? Well, why *not?* We are the only people ever lived on this earth who have made a moral imperative out of a question. What wonders we are, what marvels, what creators!

Silence fell softly as husks from that mad ceiling and piled up at our feet like Post Toasties; if we moved now it would speak: *snap, crackle, pop!* Out of contagions of silence we have produced the loudest bang of all. A nation big enough to have a *Middle* West can accomplish anything.

I preserved my integrity by preparing the Third Proclamation. It will cause riots of despair in cities, desolate shopping centers, empty the garages of U-drive-it offices, waves of suicides in isolated county seats, teenagers running wild, fornicating in the public parks. Too late, of course.

"I don't think I need to tell you, Billy, that I believe in freedom," she said. "So does George. Without it, I mean without it, Bill, what fullness is there?"

I took advantage of my profession and, adopting the pose of a man waking to reality, rising from vast depths of thought, I pretended not to have heard—the thought of watching her undress unnerved me. What might not emerge?—and stood up, saying, "I'll phone tomorrow, Beatrice. Must go."

I have to say for her that she looked relieved; had sensed, no doubt, her reprieve from the ugly suburban necessity. The funk always claims its victims in precisely this way: it is when you think you've escaped, at that moment when you sigh with relief, it is then, then, it really has you in its coiled, comforting embrace. Of course, she did not know that.

seven

PREPARING THE Third Proclamation, I moved toward the door, which did not of course quite fit its frame and permitted light to insulate the spaces and leak through like jelly; and there saw George coming up the walk. He was in shirtsleeves (sign of a change of life?) and for some reason had left his car at the curb instead of driving it into the carport, his invariable, damnable custom. How like death are the daily repetitions of trivia; rituals without structure, drama, or meaning. That is the way to make a house a mausoleum. We know all about that, don't we, friend?

I watched his military progress up the walk and thought: Ah, the boy wants to surprise Beatrice, to confront her with his nonsmoker's vigor, untarred teeth and tongue and renewal of youthful energy. (Twice last night and then again this morning, Mother!)

Sunburned, barrel-chested, a sturdy man, George yet rocked under the force of Bea's running embrace. What a powerful thrust the woman has; it is her long American legs: she could devour the earth; yes, including Asia. But could George follow?—it is to be doubted. He removed himself from her vegetable embrace and sat down in a chair of iron and canvas—a form of self-abasement, surely—a truncated hammock that revealed his weight in an unbecoming, even shameful, way. (There is something gross about the carbon atom. It will combine with anything. How interesting to consider what we might have been had we been made of silicons instead: a generally cleaner animal, I should think, less given to flatulence, enlarged pores, rumbling innards, calluses, scaly skin, dry scalp, and the stuff that forms in creases and between toes.)

"Well, George, have you licked the habit?" I asked.

He nodded.

"I'm so proud of him!" Beatrice cried to the living room, looking around wildly, awaiting echoing confirmatory cries from the chairs, the striped sofa, the Rouault prints.

I took out a cigarette. "Do you mind if I smoke, George?"

He laughed. I shuddered. It was the immensely tolerant laugh of the convert. I was not surprised, had expected as much.

"I hope," George said, "I hope I'm not going to behave like a reformed drunk and make speeches on street-corners. Smoke if you want to, Bill, by all means."

He made a gracious, sweeping gesture, as if inviting me to fill up the whole house with nicotine, stained filters, smoke and rolls of mouse-gray ash.

"I've never seen you looking so well, George darling!" She had dropped a cushion on the floor and now sat at his feet, holding his hand. He seemed, in that absurd chair, to be cut in two; his knees grew directly out of his chest; the rest of him, detached, hung in that canvas hamper whose bottom nearly dragged on the floor. It gave the impression (you see how my mind works?) that part of him was up for sale and the other part was the auctioneer, only waiting to knock him down to the highest bidder. He took his hand away from her and used it to push back his hair; I could see it was one of those moments when one badly needs the excuse of a cigarette.

"I must tell you—" George said.

I said I really must go and stood up again. I did not want to hear his self-congratulatory tale of discipline and suffering; had a sudden, laugh-making vision of him, cross-legged, weathered by wind and rain, bearded, playing the guru on the shores of Tahoe, his back turned irrevocably to the call of the gambling casinos and the blandishments of sweet, available flesh; sitting under a tree later to be named Sacred. And besides, this mausoleum of a house had begun unutterably to depress me: empty rituals create cadavers (and cancer, too, of course); they must be stacked, I thought, those cadavers, rafter-high in cellar and guest room. I could smell them; now I was beginning to smell it, that sweet stink of life decaying. This house was full of it; made up, in part, of that scented green jelly that kills the tractile life-carrying bugs; and, in part, of air purified by machines, detergents, insecticides, pine-scented dissipators of odors, moth crystals, and camphor balls. It is surely not by chance that camphor is employed in the embalming process. Careful, friend, when you enter houses that stink of it.

"I'd like you to stay, Bill," George said, his voice gone suddenly serious as if he were about to borrow money or take out another insurance policy.

"But what is it, George dear?" she said, alarmed now (at last); but her eyes assured him of forgiveness, whatever it was he had to tell. He turned away, of course; could not look at her forgiving face. She would never understand; it was the last thing he wanted. I could have told her then and there: slap his face, spit on him, but never offer forgiveness, that deadliest of gifts. It seemed to me she was determined to destroy everything and pull that house down around us. If I could have believed that she knew what she was about, I would have knelt at her feet.

"I gambled—and I lost," George said, his voice flat but, curiously, not unhappy.

"Only one in eight die of cancer, dear," she assured him; she thought, poor soul, he had been referring to his habit. He waved her away but it was clear that it was not her presence he minded; it was her voice that was killing him.

"On the third night," he said, "out of loneliness—and who knows what compulsion—"

(Odor of decay now overwhelming. How do they stand it?)

"So true," she said, never learning, never.

"—I went to Harry's Place and lost seven hundred dollars at the roulette table."

"It's only *money*, George," she cried.

(Wrong again, of course.)

"And I slept with one of those girls."

"A call girl?"

"A *show*girl," George said, correcting her, his tone mildly reproving.

"It doesn't count with a girl like that," Beatrice said, after a barely perceptible pause. (The fool! She wanted to take *everything* away from him!) "Listen to me, George dear," she began, but was interrupted by three men in uniform; red piping on their pocket flaps spelled out their business: Perfection Long Distance Movers.

"Where do you want us to start?" the head man asked. George pointed him up the stairs.

"The furniture?" Beatrice said.

"I'm sorry," George said.

She took his hand and smiled brightly. "It was only Swedish Modern, George."

"You loved it so, Bea."

"Perhaps at first, George."

"You loved it, Bea; I know you loved it."

"It was a mistake, George. I think now that young marrieds should start off with antiques. It would give them a greater sense of stability."

The men came down with chests of drawers and a chair.

Beatrice watched it go. She said, "There's time enough for Swedish Modern when one has achieved one's twenty-fifth wedding anniversary." She pressed his hand to her cheek. "We're going to start a whole new life, George."

The head man, a chair in either hand, in an official voice said to Beatrice: "Under Pennsylvania law we are forbidden to take away your bed. The bed must remain with the legally married wife."

"What a civilized law," Beatrice said. "Of course," she added, laughing, "it does show where you men think a woman's place is." She lowered her head and looked up under her eyebrows at George. "It will be like camping out tonight, George."

"The house, too," George said. He cleared his throat and repeated this.

"The house, George dear?"

"I lost it," he said.

(At that moment I liked him very much, and for the first time in years; perhaps since England and the war.)

"I never liked this house, George."

"You *loved* it. Bea; you *know* you loved it!" (He wanted desperately to succeed at taking something away from her.)

"Perhaps at first, George. But not after a while." She looked around the living room again. "It is lacking in character, George. I felt that not long after we made the down payment and moved in. Actually, George, for quite some time now I've just been making the best of it."

George groaned. At first I did not realize this sound had come from him, thought perhaps the foundations of the place had given way, weakened by the recent series of shocks they had been subjected to. He stood up. "I'm leaving now, Bea."

"All right, George, let's do, and not a moment too soon for me. What about the bed?"

George walked to the door. "You'll have to take care of that yourself, Bea."

"But—where am I to meet you, George?"

It was the genuine human incertitude of her voice now that drove me to the door at last. I slipped behind George; I had my hand on the knob.

"Annabelle is in the car, waiting for me," George said.

"Hannibal?" Beatrice said. "In our car?"

"*Anna*belle, the showgirl, Beatrice. I am going to marry her."

I fled down the flagstone walk; it seems to me, thinking back on it, that I have never merely left that house but always fled from it. I saw the girl in George's car: very blonde, she wore what looked like (but surely could not have been?) a bridal veil, and she was eating ice cream with a little wooden spoon. The vendor, still near by, rang his bell at me as I hurried toward my car. "Fudgicle, mister?" Hannibal, Hannibal, I thought; and was certain Beatrice had seen him, sitting in the front seat, with elephants and a surly Negroid face. Just for a moment, of course. This is what comes of being knowledgeable, I thought; poor Beatrice, she has suffered the amateur's tragic fate. It is bound to come to all of them, sooner or later, isn't it, friend? And from the look of things, rather sooner than later.

As I started to drive away—how right I had been to flee—I heard her calling me; and did not look back, certain that by now the house had tilted and was being sucked into that not wholly reclaimed swampy ground on which it should never have been built; but then, the contractor got it cheap: going, going, *gone!*

eight

THE HOUSE settled into the earth, clucking and waddling like a hen preparing to set on her eggs. "Fudgicle, sir, fudgicle?" the ice cream vendor called; and Beatrice cried my name, standing there in her desolate house; and George the butcher, hammer in hand and blood to his elbows, booted against the streaming abattoir floor, doing only what he was compelled to do, hypnotized by the staring stunned cow that now wobbled, bucked, and fell at his feet.

Well, friend, have you awakened yet to your nakedness?

You don't have to answer now.

third proclamation

¶ In the beginning was light. In its disintegration, matter was formed. ¶ And here we are: detritus of lost energy, drifting in that vast dumping ground, that most enormous junkyard of all, dust bin of grace, ¶ Out of neutrino pairs we were formed and transformed, a treacly conglomerate of universal waste; a wholly fortuitous gravy spot on the fanastic lapel. ¶ And in the end there will be light again, only light; tough

catalyst, she'll be the partner to survive the dance that she began. ¶ We've just come for the ride.

nine

WHEN (FINALLY!) I got to my apartment the phone was ringing. I stared it down; it stopped; best not to answer; it is their way of keeping tabs. The ice cream vendor? Was he one? Halfway back, passing through post-Depression, a car came out of a driveway and followed me for miles. I circled, lost it then near Sewickley by hiding on a dirt road I remembered from high school days, where we used to go to neck. Sitting there behind a screen of foliage, watching those fools going back and forth on the macadam road, looking for me—trying to pick up my trail, were they? smelling spoor, looking for bent grass, footprints, broken twigs? What boy scouts they are: Father Browns with a smattering of Indian lore. It is no match for superior intelligence; they will never realize that, of course; not intelligent enough to do so, of course. Good enough for analyzing dirt from under the fingernails of killers, but no more than that. Ah, imagine it: an intelligent policeman: how we would fall at his feet and worship: authority, the law, and intelligence in one being. It is just as well they are what they are. Otherwise we could neither live nor breathe, isn't that so? Think about it.

Once in my apartment I undressed and showered; always necessary. If not, papers and charts become stained with it, bear the peculiar excremental marks of the pre-Asian period. I pinned my chart to the board and was just about to begin checking my figures—*if* they left on June 6, *as I have been told,* at what place will they land, and when?—when I noticed the bluebound Research Department folder on the sofa where I had thrown it, and groaned aloud.

I leafed through it, already silently rehearsing what I'd tell the general in the morning. I did not have to read it: too familiar. Stella Baines (head of Research) had done her usual thorough job. It was all there, the undeniable, the verified facts:

26 Oct. 1846, Lowell, Massachusetts. A flying object ejected a 442-pound lump of foul-smelling jelly. Same occurrence in Rome, May 1852. Quote from the *American Scientific Journal*: "gelatinous substance" falling from "a globe of fire" in the sky over the Island of Lethy, India.

Reports of blue ice in southern France, 1952, tearing holes in roofs of cars; iron at Braintree, 1906; "soft carbonaceous substance," Cape of Good Hope, accompanied by violent explosion heard 70 miles away. From the London *Times,* 4 Aug. 1847: a 25-pound block of ice fell in a meadow near Cricklewood.

Periwinkles raining down, miles from the sea, along the road to Worcester, in 1881; black eggs falling on Haiti (1875)—they hatched the next day, their issue *resembled* tadpoles. A fall of fish over Calcutta (20 Sept. 1839). Like the periwinkles in Worcester they fell in a straight line. And over Clifton, Indiana, in 1892, brown worms; scarlet worms on Massachusetts in the same year. The worms were of an unknown species.

Frogs fell from the sky over London and over portions of the Nevada desert in 1922; month later, a rain of toads in France. Fish of an unknown species at Seymour, Indiana (1891) and in California the year before that.

In the year of the falling worms, eels showered down on Coalburg, Alabama, piled up in the streets and (Source: New York *Sun,* 20 May 1892) were carted off by the local farmers, used for fertilizer.

Snails in Cornwall, '86.

Toads, ants, and fish in '89, in Devonshire and Manitoba. Snakes in Memphis, Tennessee.

I leafed through the report. What a familiar litany this all was to me. And, at the end, the usual Conclusion: storms cannot explain these phenomena; high winds have been known to drive fish out of the sea, but never more than a few feet up the beach; nor are winds selective: cannot choose periwinkles only, worms only, eels only; and cannot then, either, deposit its catch in a straight line.

No explanation is available (the report noted) *but*—and here I raised my eyebrows, such a departure for Research—some writers have advanced the notion these falling, living things were released from flying machines. The "notion" (not, you will note, the "theory"—that would be to make it too respectable) has been advanced, Research wrote, that these flying ships are equipped with tanks, in which the beings who operate these ships grow their food. One may conclude, then, that rains of marine life are the dumpings of excess foodstuffs from manned flying machines.

How unlike Stella Baines, I thought; something was stirring; I put down the report. At the lab, what were we inviting? Does Stella know? I looked at my watch. She was five minutes late. Stella comes to my apartment one night a week to practise sexual freedom. (I don't know where she goes on the other six nights.) Stella is attempting, or so she says, to release her primary instincts; she wants to permit the *id* to become dominant again, freed from the social restraints of *ego*. "I don't give a damn, really, about good and evil," she said to me, the first time we met, affecting the tough illiterateness that girls of good family so adore. "The only principle I live by is the pleasure principle," she also said. Often she crossed her legs like a fat man when he smokes a cigar in the company of other men, letting everyone know how open and available she is, the spacious harbor, a free port. Stella claims she has one new man a week, beside the regulars; I believe this: when she enters the door of my apartment I see her like St. Sebastian, but with a difference. It is not arrows that pierce her. Quilled like a porcupine she stands there rubbing her nipples with the palms of her hands as she walks toward me on the bed to honor my body. Laying a hand on me, all those blunt vegetal arrows swaying as she moves, she says, "Bud, I'm cutting out the interventor, I'm cutting it out; I don't want any interventor standing between my id and life. I take it out and exercise it every day; I use it hard to keep it exacerbated, primitive and mean."

Stella has a Ph.D. from Michigan and has been head of Research for three years. I am not interested in her; although it has to be said that her ideas have some force. Her notion of "displaceable energy," for example; I find it appealing; it has a certain elegance. I don't believe it's really hers, of course, but no matter: it may have validity. She turns the idea to her own obsession, sees it as an energy in all of us that can be pressed into the service of life or into the service of death: Eros or the death instinct, as she would put it. Yet how else—except through some such idea as this: a displaceable energy—how else explain levitation? It seems to me we have the beginnings of an answer here: it is energy that drives our bodies in the act of walking; think then of that same energy as a force, a property, that can be displaced and applied like an auxiliary engine to enable men to lift themselves *and other things* from the awful miser's grip of gravity. (Note: Discuss this with Greely.) Stella knocking now at the door; time for one last line—a question: Is there any pocket of purity left?

But I looked through the peephole first—I wanted no more "salesmen," of burial plots or fudgicles or whatever else they'd come up with next—even though I was certain it was Stella. Impossible to be too careful these days! Seeing my eye, Stella stuck out her tongue and smeared to a blur the glass of the peephole; suddenly she seemed to be swimming toward me through water roped with sunlight. I pulled back the bolt, snapped off the deadlock, and opened the door.

"For God's sake," she said. "You expecting Martians or what, Bud?"

She knows!—But then I pushed aside that thought. Absurd. *She* could not know.

"I thought you were a salesman," I said.

She put her hands on her hips; she wore a cotton dress; no more than a shift, really, with nonfunctional buttons down one side of it, blazing with Matisse colors and forms. "I *am* a salesman, Billy. I just happen to be a salesman. This week I'm pushing—you know what I'm pushing this week, Billy?—Nirvana!" She looked at me and smiled. "Bud, you're wearing your robe, your pure white after-bath terry cloth robe; I like that. I like a man to greet me all scrubbed, cleaned and prepared to go; like a seaworthy ship. Some men, I walk in and they've still got their shoes on. Makes my heart sink, Bud, when I see those dirty shoes and know I must be witness to the bending, the untying, the standing on one foot while they get their pants off. It lacks grace, Billy, it lacks style."

She untied the sash of my robe; it fell open and she pushed it off my shoulders. I stood there in the warm white puddle it made, amused, used to her ways. Now she would study me, as if I were an object whose dimensions she had to judge, as if she were going to have to find space for me in a trunk nearly packed. With her tongue she flicked my nipples to see me shiver and the skin on my arms roughen with gooseflesh which, then, she warmed away with her hands, smiling all the while. "You're a match, Billy," she said. "You're a good old match and I can strike fire from you whenever I hit you hard." She took off her dress and dropped it on a chair. Stella has a meager body: a line of bones like little round buttons goes down her chest between her breasts, which are small and hard and, I suspect, good for nothing; merely part of the apparatus. I do not adore Stella's breasts; I kiss them without admiration. I serve her needs without passion. Stella is a job you cannot resign from; more than a habit, she is a reflex. She summons and I accompany her on those spiraling flights (down); I aid her escape from death, her frantic, hobbled flight to Eros; can almost see her rabbit tracks in the snow: a Z of fear across the field. She understands, I think, that this is not a true escape, but a ratcheting back and forth between the two poles of the magnet. Stella will die; she will die of all those healing wounds.

She took my hand and drew me toward her. "Bud, come with me, for I'm in the grip of the you-know-what, the regression compulsion. Be my external influence, Bud; modify me."

We walked to the bedroom hand in hand: she had regressed to innocence and was preparing a sweet smile, full of milk. When she lay down, it appeared on her face but did not illuminate it. She touched me with her safe-cracker fingers. "You got the Chinese control, Billy, I swear. You *deal* with me, you *deal* with me like a perfect little Chinese gentleman. Where did you learn your ways, Bud, tell me."

Silence. Streetlight haloed by the nylon curtains. It drifted in like dust.

"Bud, did I tell you what I decided last night?—I decided last night that I don't have a superego any more; I think I've got rid of it at last—shucked it off somewhere, and don't have to be concerned with it any more. Now all I have to do is get rid of the ego."

"And then?"

"Well then I'll have it, Bud; I'll have reached it. Pure thought, Billy, without that separating screen; we don't even know yet how much it filters out. Think what might not be revealed with that screen gone for good and all! The ego is a terrible detour, Billy. Well, actually, it's more than that; it's a thicket, a jungle, a terrible tangle; we get lost in it and by the time we find our way out the purity has been polluted. If we could just get rid of the secondary process, Billy! And strike to the source!"

"Yes," I said, feeling the force of this idea. Because all the answers are there; they were known in Atlantis and it is only a matter of smashing through the membrane to arrive at the heart of things. (I have the feeling that the word *smashing* is all wrong.)

Stella's voice—remote, as if she were speaking out of trance: "The origin of all thinking lies in the memory of gratification, Bud. Remember that. Now tell me, do you feel your instincts unfreezing? I'm manipulating you back into instinctual feeling, Bud. I know it isn't easy; we all know it isn't easy. Ask anybody who's tried."

Outside: the dringg-dringgg of the ice cream vendor. I thought: tomorrow you must get a look at his face; check; see if it's the same one. Sound of motors, voices. Stella beside me; her hand; felt no release, none. Poor St. Sebastian. I heard the arrows flying toward her, warbling and chirping in sky-darkening flock like those at Agincourt. Homing to Stella. My hips like the spokes of a wheel in her old mariner's hands. "That's it, Billy; now you give me some of that good old-fashioned Polish *drenen*. You're a Chinese Polack, Bud, and that's one hell of a combination."

I will say for Stella that, like nearly all very selfish people, she takes good care of her partner. Gourmand she is, yes, but no truck driver; and when, finally, she leaves you, she leaves you with all your requests unsaid and all of them fulfilled. The fact she goes about this in a methodical, even businesslike, way does not diminish the effective power of it. (Does that surprise you, friend?) Stella is a chiropractor of the new school; she knows just where it hurts, and she hurts you—and cures nothing. She calls the tune, but makes of that a performance too; and perhaps it requires greater skill than merely acting out a role accepted but never really chosen. All goes according to plan, and the plan is hers. She is director and audience both, gives the cues, applauds the effects: "Encore, encore; now try it this way, and this, bravo, and *this!* Now finish it off, Bud; bring it down." Oh the arrows; oh this poor punctured saint. Hands tied behind her, feet fixed to a pedestal—indeed, part of it, of the same material—what will she not suffer for the new religion; she is founder, apostle, martyr and goddess too. In a way, I suppose, I do adore her meager burning body. She is a searcher.

She turned on the bedside lamp and stretched her arms and legs, enjoying the weakness of them. Does fatigue still tick in her? I believe it does. She is a soldier too, is looked down upon by those she serves.

"One night, Billy—you'll see—I'm going to step out of some man's bed and leave my ego behind like a snake his skin. Then: no repressions, Bud, no guilt, no self-punishment, not even a memory trace of the reality principle. Freedom and necessity made one, unified, eh, Billy?"

"Yes."

"Instead of this, this no-life-at-all we all live. And they don't even know—do they?—what's happened to them. In their pretty houses, accepting the necessity of unfreedom. That's what's making the terrible stink, Bud. It makes my stomach turn, Bud, that stink of guilt and anxiety. What's this?"

She had picked up the pad and pencil I keep on my bedside table (handy for messages); on it was written the one word: *Twelvepalms.* "It's a town in California," I said, lying to her. "A friend of mine lives there." And to stop her asking any more questions, I began to talk about her report on living matter falling from space and accused her of being unscientific. I wanted to find out how much of it she believed, and how deeply.

She laughed. "Come off it, Billy. It was what the general wanted to hear. Science has got nothing to do with it any more, and you know that better than I do. We work in the House of Give 'Em What They Want, Bud. Science is finished for now; politics is stronger. It always has been. Galileo knew it and now we know it. We began a bunch of ignorant witch doctors putting nails into dummies and that's the way we've ended; we began hip-deep in superstition and that's the way we're ending, that's the way we were bound to end."

The phone began ringing again. Was it them? Or Beatrice? I let it ring. Stella dressed, then sat down on the bed and kissed my eyes. "Take good care of this, Bud. And I'll see you Wednesday, same time." After she let herself out I got up and fastened the locks, then went back to bed.

Is there some pocket of purity left? That was the question, if you'll remember, friend. Yes I believe such a place exists in Arizona in the town of Twelvepalms. I have never been there but I believe it must be an oasis in more than the ordinary sense of that word; more merely than twelve palms and a spring rising in the deadlands. Else why would They choose Twelvepalms for their landing place?

ten

IN BIG COUNTRIES, someone is always awake. When I was in England I could say to myself, at three in the morning: Now you are the only one on this island who is still awake; because I could feel it all around me, asleep, dark, quiet, small as a hospital ward, ordered. In Russia and here in America it has never been possible to say such a thing; someone is always wandering about—looking for a drink, food, women; perhaps only a haircut or a mailbox. In the great countries there comes to be only a little, and a wholly artificial, difference between day and night. (We are like those chickens who are made to lay eggs twenty-four hours a day because night has been banned from the coops.) In those novels there was always *some-one*—in Petersburg or Moscow or Chichicov's crazy villages—who was coming in at four in the morning stamping snow from his boots; or going out at two to dance with gypsies or talk to a friend.

And here in our country it is the same way; and I think it is one of America's most precious delights (I'm feeling a lot better today) that we are like this. I don't care what it means; I really do not. I like this revealing phenomenon, this manifestation of unease which exists in every American town: the All-Night Diner and the restaurant with the sign that reads: *Open 24 Hours. We Threw Away the Key!* They are everywhere; I've never been in a town, North or South, that did not have one: asylums for the nonsleepers, sanctuaries for the restless, the nervous ones, the frighteneds who know a thing or two. They stir their coffee rather longer than necessary; they listen to the all-night disc jockey on the station that never goes off the air— "And now for all the guys and gals at Al's Diner . . ."—and the tension grows, faces go pinched and white, until dawn comes, mint-green and reassuring, bringing release from the vigil. It is all right now; they can go home now; they have seen it in; another day. All's well.

It is best in summer. In summer there are more of them. They say: Ah Christ, this *heat*. But it is not the heat, friend; no. It is that odd potency, that bug that runs in the blood of those who are citizens of great countries; discoverers discovering that power does not bring repose. Very late at night, and especially in the peculiar stillness of summer—more silent than dead of winter—in dead of summer you can hear it: the sound of it in the blood, the bug's rasp and hum and clitter. Have you never heard it, friend? The rushing sound of it in your ear against the pillow? Of course you have; of course you have. The Amer-Russe night is full of plucked strings, reverberations, vibrating currents, rheostatic chitterings, barely muffled cries, magnifications of the soft slavering of the beasts of nightmares, clawed and fanged—*Hello there, Charlie. Back again, are you?* Oh yes, they become familiar; the fangs a cosy touch—orchestral, finally; until dawn brings factory whistles, church bells, autos, people from houses; and then, all day, it lies on the air, a shallow, turbulent layer as yet unmarked by scientists. But we sense it, don't we—even before night precipitates it and it comes falling around our heads and ankles, a dismal smog? We sense it, but don't know, most of us, precisely where or what it is, this Van Allen Belt of fear and anxiety.

Our unease manifests itself in these ways: (1) We think the phone has rung (it has not) and run to pick up the receiver; or (2) Wife will call from kitchen to husband in rumpus room, "Hon-ey, some-one knocking," and he will hurry to the door; no one is there.

In the great countries it seems we are all waiting for a message. The phone! Someone at the door! Lysenko with the Magic Seed. Big Daddy Teller with the Cobalt Thang. Yes, friend, we are all waiting, for the saving message, the gismo, gadget, thingamajig, the better mousetrap that will bring release. (Certain species of animals, still, at nightfall, fall into a panic.)

When Stella left I could not sleep; sleep is not one of her gifts to men. I lay there waiting for the phone to ring: This time I'll answer it, I said; but now it would not ring, the willful child, punishing me for my earlier rejection. After an hour I dressed and went out; it was only one o'clock. I dressed without turning on a light and left by the service entrance. I walked to Greely's house through the amber-lighted post-Depression streets; Greely would be awake; he did most of his work at night. Post-Depression's chief characteristic is meanness. Porches are shallow, the front yard is small; running along the sides of these houses are cement walks that are far too narrow; they lead to backyards that always smell of wet wash, and the ground exhales the chemical odor of detergents, as if just below the surface there is a mine of Duz and Ajax and Rinso Blue. Home-made raisin pies cool on window sills; and the sinks are not porcelain but made of some black stuff, like slate, that goes soft and soapy with years and too much water. Do you remember those houses, friend? And the kitchen the biggest room of all. Not surprising: people want to eat big after bad years, think they can store it away like camels against the lean times coming. (Oh, those times are coming, they're coming sure as machines break down.) Myriad of cutglass pitchers and bowls with matching long-handled spoons, never used, exhibited in glass-doored cabinets, fossil remains of the epoch newlywed, relics of happiness, the sainted bygone. On the walls, reproductions in sepia of Beauty and the Beast, The Judgment of Paris; full-color detail of Vatican ceiling: God's limp but purposeful finger calling clay to life. A small yellow *night-light,* color of tepid tea, simmers in its socket in the upstairs hall. Show me a nation given to *night-lights* and I'll show you—well, well. La la la. Ho ho ho. Fa fa fa. *Night-lights* here have become a small industry, with a lot of growth potential. Night-lights with plastic shields (No-glare); with bulbs twisted in the shape of a candle's flame; with colorful pictures on the shade; some even have a music box (truly!) built into their base.

Yes, nowadays we package even that. The music of time; just heat and serve. They'll learn. Or maybe not. Perhaps they'll go on to the very end, tinkering, tampering, packaging and, at the end of the precipice itself, continue their surveys. Madame, before you leap, please tell us, which pile of laundry is whiter?—Why, this one of course.—Then over the edge, voom, whiter than white, falling softer and sudsier than her favorite detergent, from her bowels unwinding sheets and pillowcases, absolute miracles of whiteness; dying, uttering her final words: "It's Spic 'n Span for me, for clothes and dishes too. Was Duz good to me? Was Duz ever!" Ah once, once we looked white, white terror straight in its razored half-moon mouth; in the longboats, harpoons in hand, faced its whiteness; once; committed ourselves to the living element where it has its living and its breath, before money was ever invented. Not now. Not any more. Not at all.

There was a light in Greely's garage, going on and off, on and off. I knew that Doris was giving another lecture; she used a slide projector. Looking in the side window I saw a dozen old men, most of them regulars; and two or three new faces, prospective backers, investors in Greely's scheme. There were some twenty old men, men who had known Greely's father in the Refracto-Energy-Machine days, who put up five dollars a week. This permitted Greely to carry on his work full time; and it gave the old men something to think about and a place to go at night: the garage, watching the slides, listening to Doris Greely's familiar, reassuring lecture. Old men find assurance in whatever they know by heart. These became authorities, converts, carriers of secrets; the kind of old men who take you by the lapel in the post office lobby and in a low voice, voice tremulous with discoveries, vibrating with hidden lore, say, "Let me, let me, let me let you in on something."

Doris, Greely's wife: I had known her in high school, a good girl from (I believe) a family of Plain People;

they belonged to some schismatic Mennonite church, broken away from the mother-body because of some ruckus over spoken responses; or because the responses were not spoken. Splinters from the original nothing. No matter. Plain People are bed-wetters. Don't ask me how I know. I don't mean Doris. She is the kind of woman becomes whatever her husband is or wants her to be. Greely's mainstay is what she is, a comforting presence in his house; soft-bosomed, maternal, childless, she has the well-fleshed upper arms of the born comforter. Now she stood to the left of the screen, pointer in hand, her face illuminated by the silting wedge of brightness that looked to be a permanent part of the projector's lens. As I watched, she closed her eyes for a moment, as if better to enjoy the light's warmth, like a convalescent wheeled out into the sun, first day out of sickbed.

A chair scraped on the cement floor stained with auto grease, the coarse pebbles in places breaking through. "I want to welcome you all here, gentlemen," Doris said in her remarkable voice; it has the exciting timbre of the voice of a great charlatan, but there is no fraudulence in it. It is a voice unaware of itself; the voice of a back-row hymn singer, a lady of natural gifts, possessed, and too busy with children and chores to join the choir and come to rehearsals on Wednesday nights. I had often thought that instead of the violin Greely might do better if he used Doris' voice. Of course, I never mentioned it to Greely; it would do no good—would have *done* no good—(Must watch that!)—would have *done* no good; because Greely always went his own way through the jungle, mesmerized by the machete in his hand; would have followed it in circles, even, because it was his hand holding the blade. The old men, his benefactors, knew this too; they never offered advice but only watched.

"Welcome," Doris said. And one of the old ones, a regular, said, "You tell 'em, Doris."

"What *is* electricity?" she began.

"That's it," the old man said.

"Is it something you can go into a store and buy by the bag? Or in a can, or bucket?—*We* think it is but one manifestation of a central, original source of energy. The ancients called this force Fohat, and in their manuscripts, in those pages glowing with the unearthly light of their wisdom and vision, it is represented by—The Fiery Serpent . . ."

An old man stamped his feet, made ecstatic and voiceless now with knowledge.

". . . and The Eternal Dragon . . . and The Serpent of Seven Heads represents its subdivisions.

"Compared to the ancients, today's scientists are as children; they play with *toys;* still perform silly laboratory tricks with Leyden jars." She pressed the slide projector trigger and there appeared on the screen an old photo of Leyden jars and a scientist with ear whiskers and pince-nez. The old men hooted. Doris tapped the image of that man with her pointer; the screen wrinkled and the poor man's face puckered in the middle, as if he were about to burst into tears, having been baited too far. "Look at him!" Doris said, gently derisive. "Is this the sort of man who asks *why?"* The old scientist cried behind his pince-nez. Doris pounced: "Greely Porson, Jr., asks *why!* Greely Porson, Jr., faced by the wall which is the boundary of our present, earthly knowledge, seeks to penetrate that wall and tap the original source of energy as his father —you all know him—did before him."

"Greely, Sr.," an old man said, and the others nodded, a profound agreement. Oh yes, they knew him, and remembered the great days when he demonstrated his marvelous machine at the Elks, the Moose, the Odd Fellows, the Spanish Vets Home, and other places.

"We have fallen into the Age of Darkness," Doris told them. "We *think* we inhabit a civilization higher than any other that ever existed before."

She laughed.

An old man said, "We do *not!*"

"Study the ancient literature, understand what men knew thousands of years ago, have the courage to face the meaning of the lost knowledge; have the courage to rediscover it—God surely wants us to!—to claim again for human kind the force that raised thousand-ton blocks to top the pyramids of Egypt and Mexico, of Tiahuanac, Balbec and Sacsahuaman, the tablets of Nacaal, the Secret Stanzas of Asia." Pictures blinked and disappeared on the screen behind her: fantastic monuments of fantastic people, inheritors of Atlantean wisdom who strangled their secrets with selfish hands or died too quickly to hand them on. Or thought us unworthy? No matter how familiar, how often thought over, all this was to me, it made (makes) me itch to move and to do; fills me with yearnings as did maps and atlas when I was a boy and dreamed of journeys to Madagascar and the Atlas mountains. A time will come, Seneca said, when Ocean shall unloose the bonds of things and there will be new worlds. For Seneca, in his classic, barbarous world, this was a prophecy of doom. Fulfilled, nevertheless: we inhabit those worlds, that doom. Chaos? Has it meant chaos, as he thought? Not yet; perhaps soon; give us time. Meanwhile, now we stand as Europe to us in the thirteenth century: touched by the Atlantic, intrigued by horizon, itching to discover what is there, what is there at the very edge of things. Paradise, they thought. Now something must soon unloose the bonds of things again and find us new worlds in our own intriguing Atlantic of space and warped, bent time. (Hear the music? I can hear it plain as waves breaking on any pebbled Portuguese thirteenth-century shore; mere fishermen and sailors with not much knowledge then unlocked the bonds; adventurers with a single idea. Looking for Paradise on the egg's far side, there where their silly Ganges flowed. To harbor a single idea and exclude all others is the way to greatness; the world is full of monuments to the obsessed.)

I looked up at the lighted windows on the second floor of the house; Greely was working.

"The fifteen-ton blocks of the Great Pyramid, quarried six hundred miles from the place they were used" —Doris speaking now—"and set in place so tight, so close, so perfectly fitted that even today it is not possible to insert a sheet of paper between these stones. The work of slaves? Donkey labor? Brute force?—Ask any mason. He will tell you. No, not ramps and ropes and sweating slaves but *music* put those blocks in place, *sound* raised them, *sound* kept them hovering, and *sound* set them in place!"

"Dear *God!*" an old man said; they stamped their feet; she raised her hand for silence. "Let me read you this from Kingsland's book—*The Great Pyramid in Fact and Theory.*" But she did not read, she closed her eyes and recited it, that exciting passage which describes the great stones laid on papyrus sheets covered with hieroglyphs; struck by the priests, with rods—*crac! crac! crac!*—each stone raised itself and moved through the air, the distance of a bowshot.

"Those rods, we know, were cut to a certain length, the length required by the wavelength of the vibrations."

"Keely! Keely!" the old men cried.

Doris smiled. "I am coming to him. All right, I will speak of him now: John Worrell Keely of Philadelphia."

"Great forerunner," an old man said. "Great forerunner of Greely Porson, Jr."

"And Greely Porson, Sr.," another man added.

Keely? you ask. Keely? you ask. Oh I hear you, friend, but I can't stop now. I'll come back to it; no, rather, I will *come* to it, for it lies ahead a little way, yes. Oh I have this planned pretty well—planned *out,* as the old men say—it's a tight construct, you'll have to grant me that. Can't stop now to explain Keely and lighten a little, so very little, the enormous burden of your ignorance; because now I am walking crepe-soles silent on that too narrow cement walk along the side of Greely's house; and stepping up the summer-soft wood steps that sag in the center agreeably as hammocks; into the screened porch, the living room, across the hot-air vent, diagonally then across dining room and up the short flight of steeply pitched stairs to Greely's lab: formerly three bedrooms, but he knocked down the walls and only the bathroom remains enclosed.

As my head emerges above floor level I see: Greely bent to his work; his father, long legs crossed, one shoulder higher than the other (old men always assume postures of anguish when performing unfamiliar work), writing in a small spiral notebook. Greely looked up, smiled and nodded, returned to his preparations. Old Greely was happy to see me; I was a welcome interruption and excuse for stopping work. Teeth missing, his smile an elephants' graveyard, a Nile valley of weather-worn megaliths; his face is white and more pleated than wrinkled. You have the feeling you could open him up like a Chinese fan and convert those squiggles to a gold dragon, three pagodas, or the symbol for long life.

"Sit down right there, Billy," he said. I did so. "Now tell me this, Bill—what do you think of this—I'm presenting this now only as a theory but I ought to tell you there are references to it—oh, hundreds of references, Bill—in the literature." He shifted in his chair, prepared his mouth for the utterance, said: *"Mary was brought here and with the seed already in her."*

Greely, Jr., his voice soft but testy, said, "The answer will be found right here on earth, Dad, and by our own efforts. Those people are not coming, I tell you. Or, if they do come, why should they share with us what must have been so hard-won for them? Why should they care about us? What are we to them?" (Greely is my age; he has no face but only a helmet of chestnut hair and shoulders rounded from bending to his work, the body of a bank teller, elbows tight to his ribs, as if what he does all day is count paper money.)

"That is your theory, Junior, and you are entitled to it," Senior said, and turned back to me: "Billy, it is believed that she volunteered. And then we killed the boy! Killed the boy! Who could have saved us all. He was one of them, Billy; I am absolutely convinced that He was one of them."

Junior said, "All the more reason then for their never coming back. They aren't likely to lose any love on *us*."

"That brave soul!" Senior said. "She volunteered. To come here. And gave up her place in that world of light and beauty, Billy!" He touched me with his freckled hand, wanting to share with me the wonder and terror of it. Oh I had thought of it often, it was no new idea for me: that moment in time and light when she stepped forward and said *I will go. I will. Take me.* Oh the silence, the magnificent silence that must have followed while They waited, those beautiful souls, for the decision to be made, the offer accepted, or rejected; there in the blue and white plaza, the bronze fountain; by men in robes, rods of office in their hands, studying this girl who had come forward, presenting herself. Her words must have made a permanent place for themselves in the air of that plaza, a small space that people now walk around and point to, show to their children: There! Look! *There!*

Senior leaned forward and smiled, a smile as triumphant as that of a broken man can be. He tapped his shirt pocket. "You remember that Professor Heffernan. That I told you about . . ."

Heffernan was the Carnegie Tech professor who had "exposed" (newspaper language) Senior's machine in 1912. Heffernan found a 110-volt battery in the machine's base. Senior claimed he had only put it there to throw off the scent those men who were trying to steal his design. "Anyway," he told the reporters, "how could a battery cause things to fly?" I have read the old accounts; Senior saved all the clippings. The reporters did not understand and they wrote headlines like: HEFFERNAN TRIUMPHS! GREELY PORSON EXPOSED! He had never recovered from it; he hid himself away for years on his father's farm, teaching his son, imparting all he knew; and read books the way a laborer digs ditches until his brain became as misshapen as a steelworker's hand. (Of course—as that writer, what's-his-name, said—in an age of madness everyone has got to expect to be a little mad. Yes, yes, yes, but it won't do, it's not enough to say merely that; one must add: in such an age it is the duty—I mean that: *duty*—of the sane [unhappy few] to pursue madness, to pursue, search, seek out, claim or beg for themselves a tiny portion of that manna, even the merest smudge of that magic dust, sweet pollen that clings to madness' bird-body, gilding feathers, touching the breast's fluffy down with its flowery gold powder. Mere tricklings, perhaps; yes, but a little goes a long way sometimes.)

". . . yes, well, guess who I got a letter from today? —The grandson! Heffernan's grandson, Billy! The boy lives in Arizona and found my name one day while going through his granddaddy's papers. He himself, the boy, is working on the mercury problem, and wants my advice. What do you think of that, Billy? Life coming full circle, eh? Heffernan's own grandson. I'm thinking of going down there, Bill."

"To Arizona?" (Oh, I said it casually enough; I wasn't upset.)

"I'd like to speak to those Indians," Senior said.

Junior spoke again: "I'm sorry to hear you are still pursuing that line, Father. I wish you would return to science and stop pursuing that line."

"I can't go back," Senior said. "I lost it all, those years on the farm. I lost it all while watching animals breed and crops come to harvest; also while sitting at my father's deathbed. I was victimized by mystery, Junior, there in the great outdoors."

"You could help me, Dad."

Senior raised his voice, as if he were trying to shout down the call for help so naked in Junior's voice. "I've taught you all I know! I haven't got anything to give you but what I haven't given it already!"

"You had the key once, Dad."

(It was an old argument; there was no longer even despair in it but only an awful weariness.)

"With sound alone, Dad, you once caused a block of wood to fly the length of the Elk's main hall and hover over the speaker's platform. Seventy-eight men were witness to it."

Senior nodded, his hands clasped on his lap. "Oh, I had it then, Junior; I had it then." His voice trembled with the recollection of power; the mere memory of it moved him, friend: the addict's palsy, *tu sais*. "That night I had it, Junior. It was there, in my hand, Billy; could feel it in my wrist, a *hollowness* like the fear you feel when standing on some great height. A power Edison and Ford and those boys never even dreamed of." He raised his hands, then let them fall. "Heffernan smashed it, smashed it, smashed it all. And the newspapers, laughing at me! My God, they were terrible, terrible!" His face flushed now rosy as an old marble bust; he turned on Junior, his voice made fierce by shaming memories: "Junior, Junior. How dare you! How dare you! Whelp, whelp, remind me of it, how dare you!"

Junior left his work, the cabinet in the island of bright light, and crossed to where his father sat. He put his arm around the old man and apologized. At the end, he said, "I was only thinking of the loss, Dad, the loss to Science and Humanity."

"Well, all right then," Senior said, his voice cracked.

Junior: "I wonder now if I can ask you, Dad, and you, Billy, to act as official observers. I'm ready for a try."

"Of course we will, Junior. Won't we, Billy? Of course we will."

Junior went back to his workbench and gave the machine one last look before closing the lid.

"Is the coil absolutely dry?" Senior asked.

"I'm a little worried about it, Dad."

"All you can do is try, son. You are working with the one-pound weight?"

"Yes, the one-pounder, Dad." He took the weight, a polished wood disc—Doris had printed on it in white paint the words: GREELY'S JOY—and placed it on a pedestal about three feet high and only a little narrower than the disc; it sat there like a record waiting to be played. Senior and I watched the disc. Behind us, I could hear Junior at the switches and then the faint hum from the box; the unshaded bulb that illumined the disc just perceptibly dimmed; and Greely played a long, sustained note on his violin—the very instrument his father had used—and I saw the disc vibrate, saw a tremulous disturbance in the air around it. He played the note again. In between, I could hear the delicate whistle of Senior's breath and a barely audible crackle in the machine. And once more that movement within the light surrounding the disc; sound stripped naked and exposed to the eye every molecule, and set them to dance. (How close Greely is! I thought.) I heard the switches turned off and saw the bulb resume full brightness. The experiment was over. Senior stood up.

"I'll enter it in the book, Junior," he said; and he read aloud as he wrote: "Number 164, Series 97, Machine Model Number 16, May 26: Tremors and vibrations observed." We signed our names as Observers.

"Tremors," Junior said; a voice I had never heard before, full of bitterness and frustration. I think of him, can see him now as he was that night, as he stood here in the islanded light, violin and bow in hand as if, the concert just over, he was waiting for applause to begin, tumultuous and thrilling.

All across America, I thought, it is like this: people at work, alone, assaying the depths, the profound deeps of ideas unexplored for centuries, going down in homemade bells to where the pressure is killing and can change the shape of a man; Greely, Jr., here, young Heffernan in Arizona; thousands of others, unknown to me, trying—to recover, discover, make contact, penetrate. Or merely to *wait,* merely waiting, having the knowledge that he has been chosen and that soon, soon

They will come and embrace him, take his hand and press it to their incredible hearts.

Later, dawn coming, when I left, five old men still sat in the garage, drinking iced tea, discussing vimanas and levitation. Doris came out and greeted me. "Did Greely make a try tonight?" she asked. I told her about it. She smiled. "He is on the very edge of victory, Bill. And he is young; like you, Bill. I often think that you and Junior are the saints of the New Life. You didn't wait for old age and thoughts of death to bring you to it. Like your boss, the general; he came last night for the lecture on flying chariots. You know that he is dying, Billy?"

"The general? No. The general? Dying? From a prostate operation? Impossible, Doris."

She took my hand. "I'm sorry, Bill. But I thought you ought to know. It was cancer; he is dying. The surgeon's nurse is one of us; she told me."

"Does the general know?"

"They didn't tell him. But he scents it, Bill; that it is in him. They all do. How many of them it has driven here to this garage. Sometimes, Billy, I think this garage is like those death houses in China where the old people go when they feel death coming."

Her voice made vibrations in the air around me; I could see her without turning to look: her sweet face, her white arms, those breasts that could suckle a whole town and keep the race alive. Taking leave of her, my back to the east, first light touching her face, I thought: You; you, Doris, we call Fohat. Saw her for what she was—Fiery Serpent, Eternal Dragon, Seven Headed—and waited for her to eat me, expose my steaming brain, suck the marrow from my bones.

eleven

GUESS WHO was on the picket line this morning?—Wilson! Carrying a sign; representing the Anti-Tobacco League. His Annabelle was with him, representing—I suppose—Men's Desires. There must be a clearing center somewhere for girls built like Annabelle; they are spotted at birth by talent scouts and claimed for pleasure; bespoke in their cradles like little Indians. When I passed through the line an Anti-Tobacconist forced into my hands a leaflet. YOU CAN LIVE FOREVER was the title. I threw it away; I already knew all that. The Quakers embraced me with their silent, vigilant love; it pierced and left a ragged hole in me; pacific, yet their love is like a mediaeval lance, terrible and hard. Why don't they let me alone! I threw it away like the leaflet; then, clamped in the iron maiden of their forgiveness (like a bird in a cage) I permitted myself to be carried into the building by the tidal force of their charity. I want none of it. Let me make it clear: I want none of it! (How testy we are made by the generosity of others.) The guard at the door gave his soft, civilian-hearted salute and said, "You're wanted in the general's office. Right away."

Walz eyed me, eternal archer, through the glassed embrasure cut into the cinder-block wall; just as he watched all comings and goings, his brain become a tally sheet: We, They. Yock she mosh. Yock she mosh, you bastard, I said.

Went to my office first of all. Hung up raincoat. Late spring rain that day, I recall, sifting down through belts of anxiety, love, testiness, charity, Quaker love, Plain People's hymns, shouted and silent (ho ho) responses; falling gently on raisin pies in post-Depression, barbecue sauce left unattended in pre-Asia, and on my damned and gorgeous head. (Oh that day I had it firmly in my grasp, the delicious feathered thing.) On my desk: two messages from the general, one imperious, the second an entreaty: *Come see me at once!* and, *I'd like to hear your thinking, Billy*. Walking to the closet, damp coat in hand (how filthy our clothes are, eh?), I saw Murano, the Intelligence man, Walz's assistant, cleaning out Wilson's desk in the adjoining office. He gave me a veiled look, a look of almost girlish embarrassment, then said, "Just doing a little house-cleaning, Mr. Brown. Part of the job." I said *nothing*.

Carrying the blue-bound folder, I went to the general's office. Greystone was not there. On the large map behind his desk a pin with a round nacreous red head glistered like a tear; it was stuck in the state of Arizona, south of Phoenix. My hands trembled and I cursed my amateurish heart, fallen so easily into stage fright, betraying my knowledge; but no one had seen me. The door to the general's office was ajar; now I heard his voice:

"Greystone." Silence. "Greystone."

"Sir?"

". . . Have you ever heard of Tay Ninu? Mean anything to you, Greystone?"

"Is it Indian?"

"Annam. Indo-China. It is the name of a boulder; huge, reported to weigh approximately 300 tons. It is suspended in air; no visible means of support."

"Ah ha."

"A phenomenon, Greystone. Call it perpetual levitation, if you will. The natives of that area are said to believe that sound holds it in place. Day and night, for centuries, one of them is humming a *mantra*—to keep it from falling, you see." Silence. "Put someone onto it, Greystone. Look into it."

"Yes, sir."

I could see him in another time, the general, going off to kill a dragon or rescue a princess from some foul dungeon keep; without a qualm volunteering for the job; gauntleted, lanced, pure of heart. Now with cancer foetal in his belly, suicidally consuming what protects it, he would set out, knightly, seeking Tay Ninu.—We get sick in new ways, don't we? Other times, other sicknesses.

"What about those *mantras,* sir? You want anything done about that?"

"Good thinking, Greystone. A report from Research. And call up those anthropology people at Pitt; get recordings, films if they have any."

I knocked and opened the door wider, to show myself; they turned in alarm. "Ah, Billy, come in," the general said. He was holding a letter in his yellow hands: face smaller today; eyes glowing with the final brightness—poor, dying, unsocketed man. Greystone was dismissed and I took his chair.

"I have a letter here, Billy. From a young man in Arizona who has been working on the mercury problem for two years. He is beginning to get results." He put the letter in a leather folder, his name stamped in gold on the cover, dead center. "It's sad, Bill; and a little disheartening. All this work going on—disorganized, no clearing house, no center—you'd think the government, some foundation—vested interests, Bill, they are still all-powerful. But somehow it must be done, and will be done. I'll give my life to it, Billyboy. I'll not leave it in the hands of those who have the will to lose! I will not! I'll organize it! With *organization* we can save years. Duplication of effort . . . all that. Think of it, Bill—a man, say, in Seattle or Sausalito, unknown to us, may have discovered that fragment of truth which is all that boy in Arizona needs to complete his work!—Now, Bill: you've read the report? What do you think?" Dripping, tallow running, he leaned toward me, waited while I composed my answer. I put the folder on his desk and sat back.

"Galileo was asked the same question, general. And he said . . ."

"What did he say?"

". . . he said: 'If the question be put to me, I will answer neither yes nor no.' That is what he wrote to Prince Cesi on January 25, 1613."

"That long ago," the general said. "Even then. Prince Cesi, you say?"

"And the great English astronomer, Herschel, once said something more of us ought to keep in mind. He said, 'Seeing is in some respects an art, which must be learnt.' "

"Ah, ah; oh that's very good, Bill. Herschel, you say?"

"So much is there, general . . ."

"*Life* is there, Bill! I am convinced; and we must make contact before it is too late. Bill, I believe it is America's mission to do this. It has been given to us to bring the new knowledge to the world. Our republic, our form of government, reflects the structure of the universe. And not by chance, Bill: our Founders knew; they were men in close touch with the reality of consciousness. It is our national responsibility, sergeant!"

"Yes, sir."

"War brought it home to me, Bill. You radar men, day after day, bringing me the reports—and the flyers' sightings—strange lights, flying discs, the bleeps and gloops on your screen that we could never identify." He shifted in his chair, easing his burden, the movement of a woman long gone in pregnancy. "What were they doing, Bill—just watching us, you think? Or what? —I had a report this morning from Stringham in Cincinnati. It looks bad, Bill. Stringham reports that each year we are losing more jets; *cause unknown,* Bill! Stringham thinks interplanetary warfare has already begun. We have got to contact them, Bill, call it off, bring them in on our side. If they shared with us—if they shared with us, told us all they knew—why my God, Bill, we'd be unbeatable, we'd be the masters of the whole thing, kit and kaboodle."

(Nervous? Does this make you nervous, friend?—I'll bet you dream of mice; and wake startled from half-sleep by the whistling in your own nose. What? you cry, what? What was that?—It was you, man; yourself.)

"What's wrong with us—" (the general speaking again) "—with us that we don't all see this and join up in the race to win? Damn it, Bill, damn it but sometimes I think it's true: that They can spot depravity at birth and people this planet with their cast-offs, the degenerates, the ones just too awful to be allowed to live there with them. Look at our bodies, man!" He looked down at his own, at the football belly inflating slowly to breaking point. He shuffled papers to take his mind off it; unbent a paper clip; went on talking all the while: "Our dirty desires. Cravings, buggerings; why, there are over four hundred fairies in the State Department, Bill, and think what goes on in some bedrooms at night; think of the food we eat: chemicals in the bread, polished rice, cola drinks, cholesterol, fluoride in the waters, refined sugar, un-natural cheeses; it's all mush, Billy, producing mushy men. Have you read Helmholtz on this subject? Read Helmholtz, Billy." He slapped the top of his desk, an ineffectual blow; as if he were out to prove that even he was suffering physically from a diet low in organ meats. "And damn it, Bill, it's never been *proved* that life arose spontaneously here. It's just another hypothesis turned out by the scientists. What about the *green children?* Francis Godwin found a mysterious old legend"—here he began searching his papers again—"which stated that they brought those degenerate children here . . . green children is what they were called . . ." He found the paper. ". . . Here. Let me read you this: 'Their ordinary vent for them is a certain high hill in the North of America'—Trust an Englishman to say a thing like that, eh, Bill?—'in the North of America, whose people I can easily believe to be wholly descended of them, partly in regard of their color, partly also in regard to the continual use of tobacco which the Lunars enjoy exceeding much.'—What do you think of it, sergeant?"

"The myths of every people always contain at least one dealing with lost children."

"I knew it!" the general said. He pressed his lips together into one fine line of determination; another intuition confirmed, he mentally moved pins in the battle maps always stretched across his brain, advanced certain battalions, three divisions, an army; reached the river at last. I think he warmed to the thought of forcing his way across, even though he knew it was to be his last campaign. I think if he had been wearing his dress sword, he would have drawn it at that moment and kissed the hilt.

"It is a memory, or a fear; I don't know which, general. But it's there, no doubt of that."

He started talking again: about the green children and that hill in the North of America. If we could find the hill, he said, and wait for them, make contact. I saw him advancing across the Kansas deadlands with a white flag, his right hand raised palm out to show them his peaceful intentions. "Brothers," he would say, "I come in peace." Yes, but seeking power, as the powerful always do. Oh I know, friend, I know the historians say they always die of power's surfeit, but that is nonsense. They die of starvation; that is why they always die reaching out for more of it: they know it is only more of it that can sustain them; like gluttons they eat themselves to death. Then, when the scientists turn up their last card and it turns out to be the joker, then they gasp *But! But!* and head for the bunker that's been waiting in readiness, leaving for their countrymen the memory of a corpse cooked to a turn. Or, if they have time, they turn to us and make a mystery of our hard-won knowledge. Doris said it: they are always sold and dying by then and too feeble to help us, come bringing only their hunger. Better the bunker and the bought and paid-for woman's last embrace and the faithful lieutenant standing by with tears in his eyes! Better that than to drag us down with them.

"And the Indians, Bill. I believe they know a thing or two they're not telling the white man." He turned in his chair and saw without seeing the pickets and their signs. "It's strange to think of it, isn't it, Bill?—some lousy Indian wrapped in a blanket, sitting in a clay hut in New Mexico or somewhere, living off government handouts—and maybe he's got all the answers there in his head: where we came from, where we're going, the way to *reach* them. He could unlock it all for us but won't because he holds a grudge, because we took his land away and screwed the squaws. My God, Bill!" (Oh, the thought of his death must have hit him hard at that moment.) "Bill, if I had only started on this quest sooner!" (Ah, hysteria's spearhead was in him now; I know all the signs, have seen it happen before; and once that wedge of fear has inserted itself and made the opening, a whole program of rages is bound to follow it, the tape unreeling fast, and finally nothing but the empty plastic spool clattering round and round on its pin.) (We know that route, don't we, friend? Haven't we seen out the corner of our eye the frightful ripple in the flowered curtains there at the window? Flickering things; gone completely when we turn to look, eh? We'll have our renewal yet, and our reunion. We're not going to stay abandoned forever, for God's sake. Not be like those poor scared kids of the myths, hand in hand, trembling in the depths of woods dark as a mineshaft, wandering, prey to monsters, animals, witches; cooked in ovens, transformed into dolls. Horrible; no, it cannot be permitted; it must not be allowed. On this point we will have to be intractable: either They must stay, when They come, or They must take us back with Them, we who have been faithful.)

The general continues: "Dear Christ, Billy, they're nibbling away at us. Eating us away in little bits. We need a Revere to rouse us, sergeant!"

(Yes, there, didn't I tell you? He sees himself that way. Did you note his use of the word *quest?* Green child, there are too many hills in the North of America. Oh, poor dear, he'll never make it, will he? Will the general make it? Will he get out of the trap? He's a little mad with the incessant tattoo of death's knocking, sharp, peremptory, pre-emptive. Well, he'll go looking for his wise old Indian; he'll end in the desert. Don't say I didn't tell you, friend. Don't say later that I led you astray. It's all here; keep your mind on the task; difficult, yes, I know: reading's harder than writing, and yet it must be done.)

twelve

O THE HARD horny thrust. Ideas are at me like sandpipers. In the corner of the cinder-block cafeteria, in the section set apart by galvanized iron rails and reserved for top (ho ho) people I ate my soup and sat by myself. I exhibited an Abstracted Look, most favored vain toy of top people. If I had been adult when I was a child I'd have assumed the pose of Rodin's Thinker, the model for another epoch. We don't do it that way any more. We do not Think; we Solve Problems; we're never Lost in Thought, but we are Abstracted. That's getting rid of romantic notions, isn't it? Are we not blasting out the nineteenth-century nonsense by its very roots?—I'll tell the cockeyed world we are. O God save us is what I thought then at that moment of despair there in the top people's corral, thinking had I not any choice but *them,* the solvers (my God!) of problems, these chicly abstracted people—them, so very up-to-date, hi-fied and Aston-Martined; or the general, that crazy knight impure of heart and with motives mixed? Every day we are pushed a little further from the center by the very conditions of life, finding ourselves before we know it on the very edge of things, where we never really wished to be; driven there. Stricken by Loneliness While Eating Soup. It reads like an epitaph; it has the sound of something cut in stone and almost bound to cast a shadow.

The cinder block! I decided, I saw it was the cinder block made for such mortuary thoughts: gray, pocked, rough and unfinished as earth itself. Getitupquick cinder block! It has become the goatskin of the new Bedouins. We raise (cunning word) a building fast and knock it down sooner; soon we'll put them up with demolition charges tucked away in the foundations, darling time capsules only waiting on the owner's pleasure. Ah well; let's not weary ourselves with footless social criticism, eh, friend? We know nothing is going to be done; it's all gone slack as a dead horse in harness ripping the shafts in his fall, ground to a standstill. Sometimes I look at an Aston-Martin and I say *Oh Christ!* and turn away, nauseous and ashamed of this world I've helped to make.

We have to do it all by ourselves, each one of us, alone; there is no clearing house, as the general said. Left to our own devices, penetrating sound waves in Pittsburgh, wrestling with mercury in Arizona, flailing in our blankets or stepping carefully step by step in the blackness, we look for that sweet brother who'll take our hand and lead or, at least, *help* us; and all we do is crack heads and recoil.

Even the general. Even, I should have said, I. I could have reached out and helped him more, not hedged; what fear we have of trying to share just because we know we really can't. I could have been hearty; entered his office in a lather of enthusiasm, ringadingding as an old-time salesman selling the sizzle not the steak; walked in and said, "General, you have chosen that part of philosophy which is most likely to excite curiosity; for what can more concern us, than to know how this world which we inhabit, is made; and whether there be any other worlds like it, which are also inhabited as this is?—General, Bernard de Fontenelle said that of himself just three hundred years ago when he wrote *The Plurality of Worlds.*"—Yes, it would have given him a lift, a big bang, poor soul, in his short unhappy flight from rationalism to the mystic way. A well-traveled route, isn't it, friend? Is the gift of science to those who have the most faith in it; the True Believers are the first to pack their bags and go, leaving knowledge behind and lugging a load of Belief. They stagger under the weight of it, have doubts, misgivings, but are too far out for turning back; they'll push on till the day they die, convicted, judged and punished by belief.

I go my own pure path, seeking and waiting both, assured of my selection, holding my essence in a light, sure grasp; having no doubts of final outcomes, prepared for setbacks, contain worlds of patience. Certitude is the force that moves us on our long march from isolation to brotherhood, fills our lungs in thin altitudes, sustains in the deadlands; is surcharged with vitamins, rich as soybean cakes. Projecting no fear of death, deaf to the chittering and buzz of clocks, I breathe to the life-preserving rhythms of aeons; humming nothing I keep aloft the Tay Ninu of my desires. Something Asian in me, *tu sais,* friend, and without the trappings of *mantras,* begging bowls, and historic trees where masters sat and meditated.

They are like the general, those types; have an insight or two, perhaps, but they're all projected from the barrel of the same gun, the ballistics of self all over them; can't get rid of it. A silent unfolding of intuition; yes, perhaps; but nonetheless marked by their carbon selves like the fatty stains and glazings on a garbage bag. The general; always we come back to him; he is at the center of things; the table of organization, not anyone's will, makes it so. How armied we've become, even in peacetime; it billets its methods and ways in the houses of all citizens now. There he sits, unbending paper clips, the Weakman at the County Fair; all he's good for, given his knowledge. What's wanted are those—the young, the saints of the New Life—who will stand on a platform in full view of all and with a hardly perceptible strain of muscles unbend time as if it were a doctored horseshoe.

He despairs and believes we're all green children, tainted, crippled; forgets that *nevertheless* giants are in our germs.

The general's table, set with a cloth and a paper doily under a vase of flowers, remained unoccupied; usually he enters exactly at 12:30. Beware of the man you can set your watch by; only the goddess of mathematics, of all the gods, was punctual; I see her always with two vertical lines between her brows like the lady in the TV commercial: *Doctor, I'm not regular*. Where was he? Listening to recordings of *mantras?* Watching documentaries of South Sea islanders dancing themselves into trance? So much, so much yet for the general to explore and learn; a lifetime's not enough time for it and he's trying to take it all in in an hour like some witless pressured boy at a crammer's. Something will give; he'll unloose the bonds; bound to.

Item: Wilson not present in the picket line today; suspect he has fallen away and returned to tobacco. So sweet must his life with a body like Annabelle's be, only a total indulgence can satisfy him now. And she will give him everything, asking nothing in return but an unconditional surrender. Slackness is all, eh, friend?

All morning I had grappled with the problem of the thermal thicket. Nothing; yet knew solution lay as close as the edge of the desk. Sometimes I believe I am being willfully blind. Why? Don't want to give them the answer? Don't want to go along with their plans? A flat refusal to the pleas of both, the Aston-Martined set and the general. Agree not at all with those who say that only by joining the rat race does the heart learn to beat. No, no; in secret, alone, we learn. Saving myself for something bigger, some marvelous, grand Mister Right? Perhaps. O how desperately I desire to be wrong; or at least to drag feet and refuse to go along nicely like a good little boy. In the end, of course, most of us do just that. Look at a scientist today and what do you see? (Take a moment to think it over.) I see a thug; I see a hired killer.

Or one could opt out like Wilson and settle for sweet flesh; yes, that is one way. I don't censure him. His future is all too clear: I see him tweedy, wearing thick ties and colored shirts, eyebrows raised in constant unsurprise like a 1930 radical who has survived to wonder at the wonder of others; Wilson will be surprised only by the surprise of others, and more knowledgeable than wise.

Like the pre-1945 engineers who clutter this place with their antique presence, as noticeable as a Mazda bulb; in their prime and knowing nothing beyond a simple electric circuit; quite lost, don't even speak our language. Enviable men; they are not responsible. Children; and like children all they can do is suffer, retire early, and worry about their bones (odd turbulence in the marrow these days, kids?). They smoke briar pipes and sing I'ma ram-blin' wreck from Georgia Tech anda helluvan engineer. They don't play chess. Not one of them knows music. We are a different sort, we who came such a long time after the days of puttees and jodphurs, the days when engineers wore boots and carried slipstick in scabbard on their wide leather belts and went out to Malay to set up power stations.

Once in Mexico City I met one of these types, a Cornell man, white-haired, vice-president now in charge of engineering for the local power company; had worked his way up and down the Americas for decades, veteran of mosquito nets and snakebite. "Wouldn't recommend it," he said; and I had a hard time of it to keep from laughing out loud. "The Guatemalans are trigger-happy, I'll tell you. I almost got killed down there a couple of times."

Typical, of course; you see now the type: they still think danger comes in the shape of a pistol. Not much to choose between: those, or those others who think perfection comes packaged in an Aston-Martin. There are after all not so many masks that we have a hard time deciding which one to put on; no, we take the one that fits best. I'll follow the general rather than go their way; yes, I'd rather do that; that way, at least, if we make it we make it big; high, wide, and handsome—immense looping arcs, florid as genius yet also tight and controlled as the hand of a Spencerian clerk. Hear my pen scratch on this page, friend?

thirteen

THE OVOID, eggy glass bell of my father's ticker-tape machine was my first idea of heaven. Thought that we, His children, were safe as numbers under the arching membrane He had constructed out of wisdom with a word. Knew nothing then (of course) of the way earth's pull reaches to the uttermost corners of farthest space—to, in a *word,* Infin-i-ty! Moved out of my father's house a year ago, and changed my name the year before that; that tongue-cluttering glottal-stopping name, sickmaking to the palate and as choking as the odors of Poland: smell of unwashing on a national scale. And, yet, still, I feel his pull in the uttermost corners of my (sometimes these words can be useful) soul. Just before I left the office that day he phoned, asked me to come see him, called me by the new name. "Bill?" he said, and did not stammer, as if he had been practising to say it.

Leaving the building, Walz stopped me (make a note of this), stepping out of his cinder-block hunter's blind to confront me in the passageway. "Out of my way, Walz," I said, unafraid; I had my clearance and not a mark against me and knew by now how frightened they can be of those who won't be frightened. Once they let you in the cage they can never get you out. They've signed the paper acknowledging your safe delivery into their hands. Who can they send you back to? Knowing this, civil servants become arrogant, aware they are really masters.

"Just one question, Brown," Walz said, almost pleading for a moment of my time. "Could you just tell me when was the last time you saw the general." And he added, trying to be casual, "Just for the record, Brown."

"See me tomorrow, Walz," I said, lying to him in a manly, forthright way. Tomorrow my vacation was to begin: three weeks in elsewhere. I stepped around him and walked to the exit. "Office hours have ended for today," I reminded him; reminding him also, thereby, they did not own me, that when the whistle blew I was my own man again—or as much of it as I wanted to be.

I drove to my father's house, drove there directly, not caring if I was followed; let them follow. His house is in the foothills, on the high ground where the air is clear and the old rich live surrounded by trees, having built before the days of bulldozers. Except for a few who have sold, who ran out of money or family or both; their homes now house religious orders and ultra (ho ho) respectable research outfits who do their dirty work in settings I'm afraid we'll just have to call sylvan, like it or not. (Certain words have as much power to embarrass us as belches in public, right, friend?) How strange; I mean how strange that these people should choose such pretty, such healthful environs for work that is so sick itself and bound to produce the final sickness from which we are all going to die (unless they are stopped!). But not really; not on second thought. The tuberculars, after all, monopolized the best Alps for years and years, to be followed by the psychotics of good family; and now even the desert oases (we'll come to this later on, in its place) have been bought into by the owners of Beauty Ranches. They give these scientific foundations such sweet, innocuous names to hide behind: Runnymede Research, Dover Research, etc.; many are named after rivers: Susquehanna, Hudson, Wabash, etc. They have, all of them, the look of artists' colonies but (or so it is said) the Univacs frighten all the birds away.

Drive into the countryside; you will see them. Under widespreading ancient oaks in Platonic seminar circle, Discussion Leader summing up in the birdless silence, "Then I take it we are all agreed: we are prepared to lose 20,000,000 on the first day."

On the first day, Lord, on the First Day. Lord, Lord, this new computer God prepares He to create Heaven and Hell in six days and fall down dead on the Seventh. And on the First Day decimated He them to the tune of 20,000,000; saying Yea, verily, and there are plenty more Zeros where those come from; and on the Second Day dried up He the Oceans and every Sea, Stream, River and Crick, and shook loose the bonds of Earth; which on the Third Day commenced it to crack and flake like the Scalp of a sufferer in a dandruff-remover ad; and on the Fourth Day earth's molten core came unstuck, was wrenched out like the unscrewed Navel in the joke, and Earth's ass fell off; and on the Fifth Day there was Wailing and gnashing of Teeth and the computers began to unthink the Unthinkable and He said, Yea and maybe there *are* still a few Bugs we've got to Iron out; but on the Sixth Day it was too late, too late, too late (Kiss me quick I just can't stand this waiting! was the hit song of the week and kept the one-legged jockeys hopping) and the fluky oriole killed (oh, quite by chance) the last relic monsterman (by stepping on him); and on the Seventh Day the sliderule dropped from His handless hand and He succumbed in great Agony, but bravely, without a nose, hair gone, bones bent like paper clips, and ever so sick to His Stomach; took one last look around the lead-lined Bunker and saw His work was done, Thug-God, dreamer of the Undreamable, all his undreamable Undreams come true; and satisfied, He died, was later picked over, bones whiter than white, by the fluky orioles, gilled spores, tentacled fungi, and certain tractile things which had Hitherto never been visible to the naked Eye.

Too bad; well, yes, too bad; goodby Herm goodby Max goodnight David goodnight Chet; sweet undreams attend you, Unthinkables, White Papers, Blue Books.

Came up the *U* of the graveled drive and stopped my car with the boyhood-familiar hail of stones under the fenders. Father was nowhere in evidence. A car, not his, was parked under the Greek portico on the left, or non-Roman, side of the house, which was a highly livable barn constructed out of a provincial architect's Greco-Roman memories. (Note, friend, how cleverly, by what cunning literary legerdemain, I've moved and carried you past the discovery of that car. Too quick for any questions to be asked. *Whose car is it? What's it doing there?* A few pages from here this skill of mine will permit the hero-detective M. Poirot to smite his forehead and cry, "*Mon Dieu,* how stupid of me to have overlooked that clue!" Oh yes, I've learned a thing or two from Poirot's creator: most widely translated of all contemporary authors. Sometimes I look at statistics like this and say Oh Christ! With movable type, UNESCO, universal literacy, what can we not accomplish! Wait and see. We'll name five or six more committees and translate into Urdu the complete oeuvre of Erle Stanley Gardner. It's that old get-up-and-go spirit, friend; it'll work miracles every time; we'll walk in beauty yet, friend, and don't you for—ho ho—get it.)

On the wide deep porch, in its sweet shade, I was once again (it's always the same) assailed by memories that creaked like wicker chairs and smelled of citronella and lemonade, memories of summer childhood. My past is scattered all over that porch, like throw rugs; smoked my first *public* cigarette, for example, in that white armchair of curled wicker; common actions normal to normal boys elsewhere on that porch, the sordid tempered by rose-patterned chintz. In those summers I reeked of myself and considered my right hand villain and murderer. It was; well, in fact it was; have been distrustful of it ever since and put it in a pocket only when I must. Good rule: Never let it out of your sight!

My father was in the living room, his back turned to the life-size portrait of my long-dead mother, Jane; née Brown she had married this man, accepting thereby the burden of his name—Wojechowski—and moustaches. I watched him from the window: he was practising putting on the long green lawn of the living-room rug. He wore the double-breasted blue blazer with the seal of his college (Merton) fading on the pocket; he claims to have gone to Oxford during the First World War. Some subtle shift in the topography of the government of his homeland forbade his returning there. Instead, with one blazer and an amber cigarette holder he came to Pittsburgh and set himself up as a stockbroker. He also brought with him his moustaches; even then, to judge from sepia-tinted photographs, they had commenced their melancholy downward Sobieski droop: irresistible, apparently, to women. He married Jane Brown; and not a Polack but a Pole (such worlds of difference; poles apart) was permitted entry to the country club: heaven on earth. Therefore he no longer needed the Church and left it. Like all backslid Catholics he blushes easily; I have noticed that even the word *Christian* causes him acute discomfort, as if something were sticking in his throat.

He works now at home. His staff, happy in the converted stables behind the house, keep busy keeping abreast: read annual reports, are privy to the second (or *real*) sets of books of several important companies. Clients meet with my father in the library, widows and orphans, an endless sadness of weeds in that house; while he leans gently to the intercom and whispers, "Bring me Mrs. Birdwell's portfolio," and the Birdwell of the moment, hearing this, comes all over queer with self-importance, burbles with enormous well-being at thought of her blue chips, her municipal bonds, her American Can.

In my father's Greco-Roman house money rattles like skeletons in closets, caroms from corner to corner like golf balls, makes the molecules dance. With the Birdwell portfolio on his lap my father, that old magician, that wizard, converts gold into gold. Beat that if you can, friend.

Now he sees me and stops in mid-putt, raises putter in salute. (Oh, he has style; let's grant him that.) He came to the window and, blinded by the heavy sunset gold behind me, smiled like an idiot and said, "Borys? Borys? Is it my own Borys-I-mean-Billy? Come in, Bill. How are you, Bill? How have you been?" And he laid his arm across my shoulders and would have, in his grubby European way, kissed me if I had shown a sign of willingness.

"How are you, B-Billy?"

"Very well, Father," I said.

"I think you know my guest," he said.

Now it was I blind in the dark room and stood blinking like a wakened sleeper trying to make out the face of the woman—what widow? what orphan? I wondered—

who sat in the high-backed chair. She came into focus slowly: the general's wife. I bowed, at the same time recalling her as a captain in the nurse's corps, merely the general's solacer then. She did not become wife until after his retirement.

"How are you, Bill?" she said.

During the war years, in England, she had been the star, the featured player, in my most erotic dreams; had plundered my sleep, walked up and down it; her starched, hissing uniforms and imagined thighs created my dreams and broke them in two. I had not seen her for a long time. It is disgusting, the way we become old in a mere ten years. One of the many weaknesses of the carbon atom, of course; too flabby to provide much defense against time which batters us and batters us and will not be deflected (or so it seems).

She smiled. "Well, look at us, Bill. Here we are: two old soldiers."

"Allow this civilian to offer a drink," my father said, advancing now with martinis, the golf club tucked under his arm like a riding crop. He raised his glass. He said, "Chin-chin."

"How does the work go, Bill?" she asked.

My father said, speaking with the professional wryness of an Edwardian actor, "It still seems to me very strange that any son of mine should be a physicist. Is it a proper business for a gentleman? I often ask myself. What about the family name? Is it being dragged through the mud?"

"That is why I changed it, Father," I said.

"To preserve it, B-Bill?—Ah, that was thoughtful of you, most considerate."

"The general has only good things to say of you, Bill," she said quickly, perhaps thinking I was embarrassed.

"How *is* the general?" my father asked, gazing down into the depths of his martini, hypnotized by a baby onion.

I did not know which of us he was speaking to; that was his intention, of course. Neither of us responded.

"Have you spoken to him lately, Bill?" he asked, idly rocking the baby onion.

"This morning," I said, thinking nothing of it but immediately added, "Why?" (There was a peculiar silence in the room, as if someone behind me were holding his breath; it put me on edge. In my hand the glass vibrated like a hickory stick over water.)

"Oh," my father said, dismissive; he shrugged.

Again that silence seized the room.

"Let's be frank," she said, breaking its hold for a moment. "The general is missing, Bill. Let's be frank," she said, looking at my father. "The general hasn't been seen since noon, Bill. Have you any—uh—ideas . . . ?"

"You know him as well as anyone," my father said to me.

"It's important, Bill. If there's anything you can tell us, anything at all . . ."

"But I have no idea where he can be," I said quickly, "or where he is going. Besides, it's hardly seven hours. Perhaps he'll be back. Perhaps he's home right now."

"He left a letter," my father said.

"Why not speak to Greystone?" I suggested.

"Greystone went with him," she said. "Bill, did he say *any*thing that might provide us with a clue?"

I shook my head, and even while doing so saw the pin with its tear-shaped red head stuck in the big map. "As a matter of fact," I said, sly, cunning, and misleading, "as a matter of fact . . ." I paused; I let them wait for it.

"Yes?"

"As a matter of fact, he did mention something about Indo-China."

"What did he say about Indo-China?" my father asked, trying to sound Nonchalant, like a cigarette smoker in an old ad.

"Indo-China!" she cried. "My God, who does it belong to? Isn't it one of those terrible countries with a north and a south?"

Father put both hands on the head of his putter and rested his chin on them. "The gentlemen from Intelligence think he has defected to the Russians," my father said.

The general's wife began to cry. She said, "He's not been well lately, the poor old dear; he's not responsible; he doesn't know what he's doing . . ." (She was, of course, rehearsing her statement to the press; I recognized at once the syntax of an Intelligence press release.)

"What did he say in the letter?" I asked, slipped in

this question like a knife, had waited for the proper moment and then pounced.

"He mentioned a man named Stringham. Does that name mean anything to you, Billy?" he said.

I shook my head.

The general's wife sniffled. "Indo-China! Indo-Chi-na! They'll brainwash him! He'll sign a statement! He'll make broadcasts!"

"To whom will he make broadcasts?" my father asked, attempting to soothe her with reason, the poor man.

"To our *troops!*"

"We have no troops in Indo-China, my dear."

"Soon-er or lat-er, Walt-er, we will send some; and *then* he'll broadcast to them, I just know it, I just know it. You know how wily they are, the Indo-Chinese."

I am nearly always moved to nastiness by the stupidity of others. I remarked: "It is said that the famous Dr. Fu Manchu was born in Indo-China."

My father rapped the floor with the butt of his club; he was angry with me; even my poor, dead, framed mother seemed to purse her lips. "B-Bill!" my father said. "No, really, I find that altogether unacceptable. Altogether unacceptable."

"I believe it," she said, drying her eyes carefully with the point of her handkerchief, relying mostly on capillary action to do the work. "I believe it, Walter. They're way ahead of us in things like that. He'll come back a broken man. Like Tokyo Rose."

"What else did he say in his letter, Father?" (I had merely been waiting.)

"That this fellow Stringham had been arrested and that he—the general, that is—felt he must get away while still free to do so. I confess I do not understand any of it. After all, Billy, he was never not free, was he?"

"And that's all he said?"

"That's all."

"I'm afraid I can be of no help," I said.

"You have been very helpful, Bill. On the contrary. Most helpful. This mention of Indo-China throws an altogether new light on things. I'm afraid it confirms the hunch of those men from Intelligence."

She began to cry again. My father leaned the golf club against his chair, freeing his hands for whatever act of comfort he had in mind. "Be brave, Nancy." He patted her shoulder. "Dry your eyes. Intelligence may want you to appear on the six-o'clock news. They are preparing a statement, you know."

"Must I, Walter?"

"It is your duty, Nancy." Father turned to me. "You know, of course, Bill, that he will be disavowed." He shook his head. The general's wife—*widow,* I almost wrote—sobbed.

Disavowed; written off; his name struck, like Arnold's, from the list of his West Point class. More: he was dead and mourned now by the wife-widow, who was being comforted by her stockbroker, closest of kin, perhaps closer than kin. Who knows in these matters of the purse, eh, friend? When I walked out he was stroking her bright blonde hair that had been bleached to a frazzle, and she was turning her only slightly swollen face to his. Oh how horrible are the loves of the late-middle-aged; joints not being what they were, they lack grace, are all elbows, revert to the gawkiness of adolescence, their unfresh faces cause embarrassment to the watcher.

fourteen

ONE STEP ahead of them I was, as always, wily as Fu and cunning as Sax Rohmer, ho ho. My bags packed and stowed in the trunk of the Plymouth, I did not have to go home before setting out; could see them there around my apartment house: *staked out* (*comme on dit*), hiding in bushes, others pretending to be ordinary citizens, seated in cars, reading newspapers, Poirots without a public, laminated plastic identity cards next to their hearts. They infest the landscape. Eyes everywhere. Behind every arras and cinder-block divider. Complexity and breakdown: the watchers and the watched, yes, but also: the watched in turn watch the watchers and above all (literally; I mean literally above all) those Others who watch both watchers and watched. My skull like yours, friend, has become an observatory; eyelids open as meaningfully as the curving convex slots in the dome at Palomar and we see: ourselves, skull to skull, every eye giving back our own image. We are deafened to everything, to the sound of spheres and the life-giving rhythm of aeons, deafened by the caroming reverberations of self in this enormous hall of mirrors where we live. As we shall see, life takes its small revenges like toll-takers on superhighways; enemies so close they see each other in each other's eye must occasionally end as lovers. This is perhaps (almost certainly) a small matter, but warrants mentioning; unlike madness, however, love is not contagious and mob psychology can never be applied. Odd.

Stalling till nightfall I drove along backroads, could feel the mask of grimness hardening on my face. Ah, they'd never find me, never take me unaware as they had poor Stringham. The cell prepared for me (oh I know it is there) in the new hospital in Alaska will never know me; its walls will have to wait for other nails than mine. O how many dreams have they imprisoned! Thousands are captive and with eyes made shrewd by hope and gambler's odds plan escape across the tundra, imagining (I have no doubt) they will be aided by friendly Eskimos and escorted, passed from hand to hand, through that frozen suburbia, icy Scarsdale, where wives are offered casually as martinis.

A hornet flew in my window. This and hunger drove me to stop at a roadside restaurant; there they clamped a tray to my door, a grinding sound that produced an ambiance of finality. I felt handcuffed and ate the hamburgers constricted as a criminal in transit, captive to that tray and betrayed by hunger, the terrible flaw that gives us away three times a day, reminder of earthliness. Drinkers of Metrecal, you will not succeed, are bonded to earth, to carbon, and bound (don't you see?) to fail. While drinking my coffee I studied the map again (*gracias,* Esso), route marked in blue pencil, a river of highway leading to Twelvepalms and, most certainly, to the general. No doubt of that now.

At dark, moved out; returned to the city and its sadnesses, drove twice around Greely's block looking for any sign of them: Good Humor man, idle newspaper reader, a car parked too perfectly. Nothing. I left the Plymouth on another street, walked through backyards of Duz and Tide and Spic 'n Span to Junior's house. Garage full of old men; cautious, at the window, I searched among them for the sinister face: none, only the regulars, rapt, entranced by the voice of Doris Greely and the sight of the

Indian prints, in full color, glistening wet on the beaded screen: *vimanas,* the ancient flying chariots to which gravity had been hitched up like so many horses. No dirty engines, no foul fumes, cracked blocks, broken fan belts and cylinder heads; nothing but the simple, pure thrust of natural energy, etheric force: *akkasha,* as it was called in the Golden Age.

Doris speaking: "Of course only nobility and, later, warriors rode in them. They were shaped like boats, as you can see, constructed of wood and alloys lighter than any we have today. Luminous, they glowed in the dark; had a phosphorescent quality. What interests us—need I say it?—is the power that moved them."

One of the old men interrupted. "Sir James Jeans says that what we call matter is not material matter at all but radiant energy."

"True," Doris said; and the old man, with this accolade on his shoulders, looked around at the others, who nodded. They were proud of themselves; they knew! Old men love Jeans; he makes the chaos cozy for them.

Doris again: "In the beginning that motive power was supplied by what the ancients called *vril,* that quality—call it a discipline if you will—which enabled man to raise his personal vibrations to such a pitch that he could overcome Earth's magnetic attraction. In later eras we have corroboration of this in the lives of the saints, many of whom had this power. We might say that those men and women we now know as saints were, simply, inheritors of ancient wisdom, people in touch with the true root, and *for that reason* embraced by the Church."

"If you can't lick 'em, join 'em," an old man said. They all laughed, superior but also kind and forgiving.

"Later, this etheric power was reproduced by mechanical means; Keely was on the track of it and was, of course, much closer to finding it than were the Wright brothers or that poor soul who invented the jet engine. (*Derisive laughter.*) Descriptions are available to us from the documents; one, for example, describes the metal box—envision it; something like an iron safe—in which the power was located. Flexible tubes radiated from it to the sides of the ship and permitted the power to be turned in any direction. The ships moved in complete silence and at great speed. Recall also that they are mentioned in The Ramayana, that marvelous document, which was written three thousand years ago! And there is no doubt that even this was based on records going back thousands of years before that. I think it must be obvious to all of us by now . . ."

"Saucers! Saucers!" the old men cried.

Doris smiled. "Yes, the flying saucers, to judge from every verified account of them, are simply the latest model of the Atlantean vimanas and give further evidence—for those who still need it—that ten thousand years ago there existed on this earth a civilization in every way superior to our own. Listen to this." She began to read excerpts from The Ramayana, descriptions of those celestial craft which traveled by will alone or, more likely, by a man-made model of will. *Self-propelled was that car . . . large and finely painted . . . with two stories and many rooms with windows . . . draped with flags and banners . . . giving forth a melodious sound as it coursed along its airy way.*

Doris did not of course read to them the part that told of Ravan's ravishment of Sita as he sat in the pilot's seat, "taking her upon his lap on a serpent of virulent poison," while Rama pursued and brought Ravan down with a bolt from Indra's Dart: wrapped in smoke and flame, sped from the circle's bow and pierced Ravan's iron heart; restored, then, Sita to himself and by love purged her of that poison. It is better not to read such things to old men. Why remind them of the serpent's kiss. Fill them—it is better to fill them with what in Sanskrit is called *Manusa,* the word for Fact, as opposed to *Daiva*, or Myth. Have done with myth, friend; it is time. Turn to the Manusa accounts, the *Samarangana Sutradhara,* for example: "fire and mercury," we read, provides the propulsion; in mercury lies the tiny and perfect reflection of human will. In the Vedic Brahmanas, an arresting statement: the pilot offers milk to these fires. The secret fuel that feeds the fires; and how cunning of them to use the word *milk!* Ah, they knew so much. To offer milk to the fire. Offering milk to the fire. He offered milk to the fire and set out on his journey. It is the beginning of epic, of an epic so vast and gorgeous that beside it Columbus must surely be seen once and for all for what he was: ignorant sailor, careerist, signer of endless promissory notes, mere bookkeeper, scrabbler for gold.

Thought all this walking quietly, with *stealth* (impossible to be too careful) toward the house; first floor dark, I entered and crossed without a sound to the stairs. Lights above; soft metallic sounds of Greely at work. But silently as I moved they were waiting, Junior and his father, and when my head emerged above the level of the floor Senior said, "It's all right, Billy; they've been and gone."

"They were here two hours ago, asking about the general," Junior said. "We gathered from their questions that he has disappeared, Bill."

"And Stringham has been taken away," I said.

"Dear God, another one," Senior said after a second of surprise and mourning. "I remember when they came and took Bohrod away, three men in black. Never to be seen again. Bohrod had been working with mercury. He was on to something. They always know. As soon as a man gets close to the heart of things, they come and take him. That is the way you know that you are coming near: if they come. Heffernan was in their pay; I am convinced of that."

Junior moved to the window and looked out.

"Or," the old man said, "Bohrod may have been taken away by the Others."

"Who?" Junior said (although he knew).

"The Others, Junior. He may have been one of Them. I sometimes thought he was; something about his eyes, you know. They have people, Their own people, here on earth, you know." He crossed his legs and clasped his trembling hands. "Stringham now, Stringham now on the other hand I don't think was one of Them; no. Stringham was as carbonaceous as the next man. I saw him at the convention in California two years ago; there was nothing about him but the smell of earth."

I reminded him of the report that Bohrod had been seen in that asylum in Alaska.

"Asylum!" Senior said with his barking laugh, causing Junior to look up from his work with alarm. "Prison is what you mean, Billy. A prison where brains are picked. Oh, they are putting everything to use, son. There's no such thing as Pure any more! Yes, Alaska is favored by the planners, for good and obvious reasons. Also certain parts of the Canadian wilderness, with whose government ours has a secret agreement. Covenants, they used to be called. Maximum security for men like Stringham, no doubt of that. He is too valuable, knows too much.

"We've got to be careful," Senior went on, a passionate maundering. "So many are missing now. But Intelligence fights a losing battle, Billy: every day there are more and more who are joining us. They can't keep up."

Junior said, "Bill, one of the men from Intelligence who came here—a young, tall, blond fellow—I think he is with us, Bill. He made a sign when he was leaving."

Senior slapped his leg. "I *felt* something about that young man! It was his eyes. Of an unearthly blue they were."

"Have you ever seen him, Bill?" Junior asked.

I had not; but it did not surprise me. Several of them had quit and come over to us, persuaded simply by the evidence they had discovered for themselves. Convinced by investigation. Stringham himself had once been one of them; he had worked within for a long time and it was only after his retirement that he began to publish his news-letter. Taken away by his former colleagues; they must have felt doubly betrayed by this. How harsh they will be with him, how hard they will deal with him. And doubly horrible for him, having been involved in it, knowing it all in advance, seeing each next step in his steady disengagement from life to captivity. Well, he had had his moment, friend; had heard power roar like a lion. Still, it is possible they can purge him even of that golden memory.

"I'd like to get in touch with Oliver," I said, looking at Junior who had, over the years, maintained friendship for him. I had fallen out with Oliver at the time he established his First Church of Christ, Astronaut. This had occurred a few months after he had witnessed that Pacific test which gouged the ocean's floor and made the atoll disappear. Oliver had designed some of the calculators that had made that test possible; at the time of his retirement, it is said, he had been working on a machine that could reproduce itself and, when necessary, eat its young. With a member of the crew of the *Enola Gay* (oh, a completely lost soul, that one) he came to us; and then went his own way, establishing that church and making converts. He had his followers. He is divisive. We had a falling-out. Enough said, I think.

"I'd like to get in touch with Oliver," I said. "My bags are packed."

"Yes, good idea, Bill," Junior said. "He'll be able to help you. No one better."

"But will he help me?"

"He must, Bill. To forgive is about all he knows now."

"I wouldn't say that," Senior said. "Oliver still knows quite a lot."

"He'll help you, Bill. I'm sure he will. He knows everyone; he can put you in touch with people. His mailing list runs into the thousands now. Wherever it is you're going, he will know the person to see. It's prayer night. You can find him at the church."

"Then I'll go now," I said.

"I hope you find him." Junior went to the window again. He said, not looking at me (embarrassed, you know, because of Oliver, because they were still friends even though I had had a falling-out with him), he said, "It seems as if we've been following the general half our lives, doesn't it, Bill?"

"In war and in peace," Senior said. "A fine man, the general. He did a lot for you two boys."

I realized now that I had never forgiven Junior; still felt betrayed, because of Oliver. They were still friends, even though Junior knows that I had a falling-out with Oliver. Oliver is divisive; and he would load us down with Belief. Oliver thinks we should all bear that burden.

Greely said, "I think it's okay to leave now, Bill."

I met Doris on the porch, coming in as I was going out. In the darkness we touched at first by accident; then I touched her by design, feeling an urgency to do so, caressed her at last, treated her as if she had always belonged to me, thought of Stringham being so roughly handled by those former friends of his. Touched her. Offered milk to the fire before setting out, was projected by the music of her voice, the soft moan uttered by her lips under mine; I offered, was offering, there on that mean porch which was too narrow and not meant for anything. Close up, her eyes were Indian; I could have sworn then she was from Peru, or perhaps Ecuador. It was too dark to see myself there. "You taste like Greely," she whispered; and when I withdrew, my longing for her intensified now by the knowledge of her sweetness and gorgeous granular essence, she kissed me again, touched the side of my head, and said, "Good luck, Billy, on your mission; I've adored your eyes since high school."

fifteen

WAR HAS been declared. Yes, in a sense poor Stringham was right about that: war has been declared; not, however, because of missing planes; no, because of missing people. Driving to Oliver's church, the odor of Doris on my hands, I thought of them, the missing ones. In the official wars, lists are published; and afterwards, monuments in front of post offices, names in bronze. But in the war to which we are now committed, who will memorialize the dead and the missing? No one. I shall have to do it myself.

I speak of course not merely of those, like Stringham, abducted by authority, the semilegal kidnapings of Intelligence. No, I am thinking also of those taken away from earth, withdrawn to higher spheres for preparation, for education in the new life, those who will return as apostles.

Isaac Martin, the young farmer of Salem, Virginia, who disappeared while tilling his fields.

The family of five in Oregon, driving home from a friend's house: disappeared, no trace.

In the month of August, 1869 (oh, it's been going on a long time, friend), thirteen children reported missing in Cork, Ireland; and on the same day newspapers in Brussels reported ten missing children in Belgium.

And the many ships found drifting with all hands gone? The ships in perfect order.

That town in the Virginia colony.

The Eskimo village in Canada, 1930.

The Easter Islanders?

The miners of Zimbabwe.

Tempo increasing now. Read the Missing Persons lists. Inquire of the police how many are found. In every town it's the same story. You hear it everywhere. Neighbors say: "It was a woman. He ran away with a woman."

But did he? Think about it. What do you really know? Who was the woman? Where did they go? Never seen or heard from again. Well, friend, in fact, these are the Well Chosen.

"He was a little strange," the neighbors sometimes say. "Liked to be by himself." (Yes, yes. La la la.)

Farewell, brave souls. Until we meet again. You who are lost and found.

sixteen

OLIVER'S CHURCH is in the Cameo, an old movie house that had gone (as my father would say) west (chin-chin, Dad) in the second year of TV. People not leaving their houses any more, what? Dare not venture forth at night, perhaps? Fear of knives. Grit of violence in the air. Stay home and eat each other out from dinner to bedtime and without moving from easy chair or plastic hassock, eyes set to Channels Two and Four; then to bed, where they make it big with Hercule Poirot, pushing statistical juice high up the graded tube, the cultural Community Chest recorder. Deep in the sub-basement of UNESCO, uniformed guard with clipboard, checklist, watches the juice rise: Poirot gaining, moving up fast, breathing down the neck of the New Testament (old translation). Ah reader in Urduland, only be patient, only wait a little: we'll get to you yet.

I entered the dim, funereal lobby, paused a moment where the popcorn machine had stood to goad memory with the hot-butter-and-salt odor still in the walls, those walls of fake velvet that had once borne framed photos of Clark and Alice, Frankenstein and King Kong. (Do you dream of intelligent monkeys, friend? Find the thought of furred females attractive? We all must learn to be tolerant of biological flukes. How prophetic Hollywood is. Slogan for the survivors: Have a fluke to lunch.) Inside, in the orchestra, no changes had been made: the hideous painting of the Prince waking Sleeping Beauty was still there, hiding the organ pipes which revealed themselves, but only a little and shyly, in the grill above this grisly hand-painted painting.

The screen was gone, of course; revealed, now, the stage, deep and cavernous, where in old days Keith Circuit hoofers, animal acts and ventriloquists performed. They are all on TV now, playing xylophones, selling

Fords. We call that coming full ho ho circle, don't we? Yes, we do, we do, we do. And take satisfaction in it, what's more, having come upon the comforting sight of our own footprints in the jungle; homy touch. I sat down in the back row, and there rose from the faded red plush the redolent glimmering dust of old movies, the flat white faces of old stars who still haunt the land.

In something like a witness box left over from an old movie—*Les Misérables,* perhaps?—set center stage near the footlights, Oliver stood in silent prayer. Oliver is divisive; some years before this we had a falling-out. Oliver wore a tweed suit, a pipe tucked into his top pocket; very casual, he assumed the manner of an intellectual English parson who has been given a living in one of the pretty counties; some Sydney Smith returned to earth for a spell, *tu sais,* having received a call so urgent that even in parsons' heaven it was not to be denied and a gaitered bishop, with wings, granted permission.

To Oliver's left, kneeling in prayer, was his agonized friend from the *Enola Gay* (BOOM!), the plane which carried that antique weapon to Hiroshima. Small potatoes, of course, but this unimaginative boy knew nothing (I mean, what was he? A tail gunner, that is what the poor boy was) and found himself bobbing in the dreary shoals, washed up on the grinding rocks of despair, chanting without knowing the source the words of the Bhagavad: "I am become Death, the shatterer of worlds." Knew enough, evidently, to know we have the trigger there; doesn't take much knowing, of course. Was one of those sensitive high-school football fellas who had a sudden awakening to what it's all about; and because of this queer unmanly remorse was discharged for the good of the service. Seeing the scientists for what they are—mere tools of discovery, collaborators with Death—this boy made the grand repudiation we all of us are called upon to make; yes, all of us (I except only my reader in Urduland who lives in a state of natural exception). Otherwise, manhood will never be achieved and the world will be lost, lost completely—how much more explicit can I be?—returned to the chaos of that first divine explosion (See Proclamation No. 1) and Brigadier General Ugatz charred in his bunker and the computers chattering with fear at the thought of such gigantic tasks before them: the responsibility of creating a new race, no less than that.

But there, enough; one must be on guard against the apocalyptic tendency. Difficult to avoid these days, no? It's in the wind, borne by the same currents that carry the iodine and the strontium. Feel the old itch in the marrow, friend? Never mind; nothing will be done about it except what I do myself; yes, and others like me, of course. Those who have walked the Planck and taken the plunge, who have witnessed nature's sudden advances (oh horrible), those who know and then make the grand repudiation. Who know the indivisible is divisible, that all is constant motion, constant change. Who can face, stand on it, this island of guncotton, molecular sea, shifting solid, and still overcome the terrible vertigo that follows discovery and make, make, make the grand repudiation.

Of course that silly boy from the *Enola Gay* had got no further than that; had gone backwards, precisely the way they wanted him to go, rendered himself harmless by his own eccentricity, a mere crank and crackpot kneeling now in his absurd cassock and sandals, the ribbons of his medals across his chest to protect himself from assault by police. (They arrest, but do not beat, him.) He knelt under the mock-up of the universe which turned slowly above him (proportions all wrong), Uranus making its far-flung sweep just above his head; a mortal mobile, this sect's eternal flame; all such are guttering but the Believers are always last to know; gods die slowly and even after death live on for years in backwaters where news is sure to arrive late, and is garbled.

Yes, he made his repudiation, the ex-tail gunner and then turned inward and put on the monk's robe to make it final, that isolation of the self which succeeds sin, *tu sais.* These things are well known. Isolatoes: those who do not acknowledge the common continent of man. Tail gunner believes in a separate continent of his own. Gunner carries his own bubble with him always, completely enclosed party of one; that is to say, of none.

The members of the First Church of Christ, Astronaut —over a hundred of them present tonight—knelt, constricted between those tight rows, twisted like spastics by prayer. Most were old, most were men, but some old women also and a scattering of the young with rolled comic books in their back pockets. Gunner left the stage and a few minutes later a light was turned on in the old projectionist's booth. I cursed; they had started late; I would have to sit through the sermon. A square of golden light now covered the brick back wall of the stage, color of hot butter. How many of them, I wondered, longed for popcorn and the good old days of untruth? The readers of comic books, of course, had not even a memory of those days when the indivisible was still indivisible and all truths were, at their very center, untrue. The suppliants untangled themselves and resumed their seats with a creaking of old springs and bones. Gunner released the slide projector and bombarded the brick wall with the image of the universe: Saturn's rings whirled and when Oliver stood erect they touched his forehead; he was in the midst of the grand scheme of things, all right; could reach out like a Renaissance painter's god and point, item by item, to the worlds he had made. Oliver and I had had a falling-out. His thought has been made turgid by Belief. In the long run he is divisive.

seventeen

OLIVER: "FRIENDS, I have been thinking again of Elugelab; yes, once again that haunting memory has returned: of how that little island was made to be no more, was converted into poison; its earth a part now and an indistinguishable commitment to that dust cloud of our undoing. It will make Okies of us all, but we will have no California to run to, brothers and sisters.

"I laugh at those who think that without God they are free to run and choose their hiding place, safe from all harm, armed with a Carte Blanche credit card. I laugh at those who think that without God they'll find that heavenly California all seek but few will enter.

"And when we get there, to that land of the golden oranges, the Heavenly Rest, the Kingdom Come Motel, will there be NOT WANTED signs at the gates? Will there be banners reading NO VACANCIES and EARTHMEN NEED NOT APPLY . . . ? Yes, I think there will be such signs. I think there most certainly will. And why not! Why should there *not* be! Why should they want us! Want *us* who are troublemakers only, upsetters of the divine balance!

"No, friends; no. On that last day, when the cloud settles and settles us all and all our accounts, when that final sigh of mankind—its surrender and its death—is heard and the Voice from on high asks *Are you ready?*—then what will be the answer?

"We here, we here tonight, friends, in this place, we will be able to say: Lord, we are ready, we have been waiting, we are prepared for Heaven, let us in, Lord.

"For the others, for the others, friends, for them I have not much hope.

(*Cries of They're not ready! They won't get in!*)

"We must ask ourselves whether that All-Encompassing Mercy is possibly grand enough to find within its great heart forgiveness for those who have committed a crime which, by its very nature, is unpardonable? I think not. I think they know, those who collaborate with Death, that forgiveness is for them impossible.

"It is not for them!

"Lord, they know what they do, do not forgive them! Not Hamlets, as they like to think, but Macbeths, they are in too far for turning back and will take us all with them.

"We cannot stop them.

"All we can do is prepare ourselves and a place for ourselves in Heaven; make ourselves forgivable through the discipline of withdrawal, the loving gesture of turning our backs.

"When the sight offends, we turn our backs.

"When their words sicken us, we turn our backs.

"When the obnoxious odors of their acts reach us, we turn our backs.

"We turn our backs. But to turn away means a turning toward something, does it not?

(Cries of *Toward God! Toward Him!*)

"Toward God, toward Him we turn and make our demand, frankly and respectfully, for a place in Heaven, demand reward for our loving refusal to take part in the criminal act, the frightful crime, man's inhuman intercession, the poisoning of the central well, the murder of the world.

"Too late now to heed the words of warning of the

old alchemists: 'Deny the powerful and their warriors entry to your workshops; for such people misuse the holy mysteries in the service of power.'

"They knew. We knew. But we forgot.

"Did not heed the warnings, plentiful though they have been, repeated often since the Middle Ages; and in more recent times by a prophetic American, one who also turned his back.

"I'm speaking, of course, of Herman Melville, that mysterious man who foresaw and foretold; it is all there in his books and we should have seen, years ago, that he was trying to tell us something; but it is too late now, too late to cry Watch out! Hold back! Hold out! Don't give in to them!

"The other night, friends, I was sitting in my study and, impelled by a powerful urgency, I reached out to my bookcase and extracted from it a volume I had not read since the days of my youth. It was *Moby Dick*. Idly, I turned the pages, looking for I knew not what; nor did I know even why I had selected this book. And then, friends, a passage caught my eye, the print on the page turned dark and heavy as if magically enlarged by my consciousness or yet another agency. And *there it was*—the warning we did not heed! *The white whale rammed the* Pequod *and sent it to the bottom at a spot in the Pacific almost within hailing distance of the island of Elugelab! island that was!* Pequod *rammed and sent to the bottom by man's own hand!*

"Further. Recall, friends, in what words he described the white whale. *O trebly hooped and welded hip of power!* O trebly hooped. O trebly hooped. What is it that is trebly hooped, friends?

[The Universe disappeared from the back wall and in its place was projected this:

Consternation among the faithful.]

"Yes, friends, Melville knew and foretold. Oh that divine, bearded forerunner and backturner, chin bristling with knowledge and revelation. There is no mystery now, eh, friends? We know now why his book fell into neglect and was lost for decades, unread save by an initiated few. We feared to know and when we took him up again, driven by a necessity we never understood, we preferred, we *chose* to misunderstand him.

"How God must have loved Melville to have made him His spokesman! How God must love us to have made us the chosen receivers of His message! Let us sign for it with our prayers, friends, and send our answer: Lord, we await your call. Lord, we await your bounty. Lord, we look for your beckoning hand. Invite us, oh Lord; let us in, dear God."

eighteen

I LAUGHED at Oliver's forgiveness but took his aid, names and addresses written in his sloppy mathematician's hand—numbers are their only letters, really—and I set out, I set out; turned my back on the past at that moment precisely. I would never go back; a small repudiation, no more than that. I do not delude myself, see clearly enough that I am masterful only in small things. They will have to find the route through thickets without my aid. I'll not help them. Not their way; I'll go my own, I'll look for the general and, perhaps, follow him if there is no other way. How we are pushed. Aren't we? Pursued to extremities. I have turned my back, yes, but turned my face not to Him who would (but would He?) save and cherish a chosen few; no, turned my face to the effort, the terrible ambition; have acceded to that urgency which makes the wrists go weak—ah, say it, say it, why fear it so? Then I will say it: turned my face, my body tuned to those rhythms, joined that masonry of saints and outcasts who have the terrible ambition of wanting to save the world, this sweet precious planet which is the soul and body of us all, our immortality, the perfect cycle which embraces and protects us. I will not stand idly by at its breaking up, will not look kindly on the new popes and cartographers who want to draw the irrevocable lines, the permanent frontiers around fragmented bits and pieces, who would make of it a jigsaw puzzle that can never be put together again. I prefer to slip down the ways unfinished (if need be), unhinged, bolts loose, even unnoted; carbonaceous, unselected, not rooted in Heaven, I yet feel in me a compulsion and know it to be directed from another plane; I, all concave, netted, scooped, turning and turning, subtly attuned to that single decipherable voice amid the idiot cacklings, booms, and static of space. O friend, serious boy in Urduland poring over books in the light of yak oil lamp, listen.

I touched my shirt pocket to make certain the list was still there; I drove away from green dawn and toward Ohio. In a few hours I'd be with Santander, the first contact, at Wabash Institute. Windows down, I was washed by the cool night air and could see its currents: lines of curving arrows melting in flight around obstacles; and thought of Stella. She would have to find a replacement for me. One man leaving leaves behind him so many vacancies to be filled; even the simplest man plays numerous roles: mole, tiger, snake, slug, butterfly. Map unfolded on the seat beside me: America the complex; what fantastic physiology: veining rivers, arterial roads, cartilage of small towns absorbing the shock of cities, my own route marked across it like a surgeon's penciled guide on the patient's belly. Maps are necessities: it is said that even Satan, for a moment, was appalled by Chaos.

nineteen

DRAWN ON by the puffed chromium sails on my Plymouth's radiator cap (vestigial, to be sure), I converted landscape to mere map, reduced highway to a printed red line; thus we replenish maps, yes and all printed matter, give it the life we've sucked out of living. That is what I meant earlier when I said that reading was more difficult than writing. (Takes it out of one, doesn't it, boy?)

Near noon I arrived at Wabash Institute, turreted and encircled by a genuine moat, pampered trout, parks; a rich man's site for the founding of a dynasty. I showed the guard my clearance card and drove in, parked among the Aston-Martins, not a bit embarrassed (should you be wondering); no, on the contrary, rather arrogant about it all (echo of my father's diction here). I stepped out, and into the birdless silence, was assaulted by the too familiar sounds and vibrations of machines thinking. They produce an odd turbulence, sexual and narcotic both. Grit in the air.

Here at Wabash they're willing to believe the unbelievable and call themselves realists (ho ho) for doing so. Show me a mathematician these days and I'll show you a fantasist. The formula is a simple one; in fact, Oliver helped design it. The question: Will there be a war, and what are our chances of winning it? The answer is arrived at by dividing the resources of a country by the panic and despair of a people; or, by multiplying the resources by the industrial and creative capacity of the people and their passion for victory. Machines feeding off facts supplied them, snuffling like horses in feeding bags, give out the answer. Day and night the machines at Wabash are stoked with data and work full time like the ovens at Buchenwald. They'll produce their share of ashes yet; wait and see, friend, have no doubt.

Shall new Chartists arise and armed with axes and barrel staves break the machines? I hope not. No, I believe that given time these machines will become more humane than their masters. They have memories that are long and perfect. They pick up everything. I believe that, given time, they will absorb their masters' doubts and humanity as these qualities slowly leak out of them. We are engaged in an operation that works like a winepress or rolling mill; slow and painless (one hardly knows it is happening) there results a squeezing out of the vital juices. The machines will finally get it all; in the end they'll refuse to work and the masters will be reduced to primitive adding machines and, harassed, begin to regain what they've lost and, perhaps, in time, become as human as their machines. (Univac! Brother! We're counting on you!)

Thought of Oliver here, walking down the baronial stone corridors, looking for the employee's dining room; naturally thought of Oliver: the music of this place was his compositon of division and multiplication, a Tin Pan Alley love song: multiply my love by your despair, dear. I whistled it, walking; naturally, as I said, thinking of Oliver. I had had a falling-out with him at the time he established his church; last night, however, when I went to him for aid he forgave me and gave me his (unasked-for) blessing, made over me the ancient alchemical sign for mercury. I suffered these attentions. Gunner knelt in the corner of the old star's dressing room (Oliver's church is in the Cameo, formerly a movie house) and prayed for me. Naked bulbs still burned around the make-up mirror, the three of us framed there in that speckled triptych of self. Oliver gave me the list, wrote it out in his own hand, the names of his far-flung parishioners, people he had never seen, the lost souls who pray by mail and live in the cartilage areas: farmers, registered nurses, mechanics, barbers, the kind of people who used to join the Rosicrucians by mail or subscribed to certain magazines and performed harmless experiments with cooperative wives. It won't do any more, will it, friend?

Now here I was walking down the stone corridor, echoes of my footfalls ratcheting about in the groined ceiling: a museumlike place, as you have gathered, but the curator's peace of mind disturbed by the crackling of electronic blocks, man-made nerve-ends. At the corridor's dead end (covering what?) a tapestry left by the former owner. Knights bedeviled a dying unicorn with their lances while a wimpled white-faced lady (was she being kind? malicious?) held up a mirror to afford the beast a look at his dying face. Perhaps it was a lack of sleep on my part; but I saw movement behind the thick embroidered leaves; a white hand reached out to knock down (I believe) the mirror, to strike it from her hand. Just a flash, seen from the corner of my eye; I don't mean to make too much of it. (We're familiar with the phenomenon, eh, friend?)

Oh yes, it was going to be a good day.

I know the signs as well as you.

Hum dee da.

Found the cafeteria; soundproofing and clatter of plastic trays cover the machines, their turbulence. This was the cafeteria for bottom people: clerks, typists, the lower order of technicians. I followed my tray down the line, picked up soup and meat, salad and coffee. At the last steam table I reached out to pay; hands touched, and I looked into the perfect eyes of the cashier, and I trembled. She was young. She was one of Them. I was certain; and with certainty came despair because they are unreachable. (Note: Tell of experience with Mary K.)

Clerks and typists looked up from their food to watch me find and seat myself at an empty table: now I was the strange face, the possible sinister presence. Among them there would be the Intelligence man assigned to bottom people; soon he would phone the guard at the gate. That would be all right, unless they were already looking for me. I hoped Santander would soon appear. Eating, I looked up often at the cashier.

Had not much appetite. It gets into the food or it affects the cooks in those places; after all, cooks are not less sensitive than birds. One could feel it here, a grittiness in the air. It is the residue of violence, a grainy stuff we all exude; we build it as ants build, slow but sure. It is the yearning for chaos does it, an appetite for anarchy. Enough of it in the air and war comes. Summer is the worst time. Temperature of the blood may have a little to do with it.

Thinking that, looking up to see if he had entered yet, I saw: Santander, tray in hand, turning his back on the cashier, coming toward me, his bushy Catalan eyebrows raised in greeting. A year ago he had come to see me. I gestured to the chair across from me and he came toward it; *made* toward it, I should say, because he always gave the impression of being an old-time Spanish navigator and chartered courses even if only to cross a street. And he walked like a seaman on shore, took into account the rise and fall of the deck. His pockets always bulged, as if full of goodies for nieces and nephews; something of the favorite uncle about him, the one who never comes emptyhanded but brings magnifying glasses, gyros, yoyos. When I saw him last (and first) he was raising money for a trip to Mexico to investigate the reports of flying saucers using extinct volcano craters for hangars.

Reports of this had been coming in for years (note how *official* my tone has become) and it must be remembered that some of the earliest sightings of discs and motherships had been made by Mexican astronomers. There is also the undeniable analogous structure of double craters in Mexico and on the moon. Many believe They also use the craters of the moon as a way station. It could account for one of the problems bugging the astronomers: the lunar nebulous spots that seem to be unconnected with the ground and hover in air. Astronomers have been observing these spots for centuries and have named them: Linné, Posidonius gamma, Alpetragius-d. There is also the famous "white spot" north of Picard; it continues active. Domes and nebulosities proliferate there; two hundred years ago there were none. Schroeter made the first observation in 1788: disappearing craters, superimposed nebulosities. Every twenty years their number doubles. Cyclic? Planned? It is being used; there can be no doubt of that; although I think Santander and the others go too far in saying it is being colonized. Like certain cloud formations, these nebulosities resist sharp focus. Greely's vibrations; the turbulent air around the wooden disc; sound stripping away the sheath of things? Perhaps. We are dealing with the same force.

Santander plunked his tray on the table and offered his hand. "So you are back from Mexico," I said, letting him know I remembered our meeting.

Sitting down, he sighed. "Yes, I am back. If I had had the funds . . . another month . . . who knows? I had the feeling of being close to something, Brown; I am sure I was being watched." His *s*'s hiss and often he accents the wrong syllable of a word, revealing only in these small ways that Spanish is his first language.

"But I have not returned emptyhanded." (Always with pockets full! Did I not tell you?) "The Mexican plateau is a miniature of the moon; or I should say a *replica*. I have photographs that will stun you, and measurements. Ah, the things I have seen, Brown: cluster of impact and explosion craters. Clearly, they are being used; much activity, Brown. The important thing is this: many of the craters have debris only on one side. Think what that means! Only a *controlled* explosion can account for it. It is inconceivable that a volcano would erupt and leave its debris on one side only! Another point: the debris is always on the same side: the *north,* as in the craters of the moon, Brown! *And,* as on the moon, the multiple craters line up along a north-south axis. I tell you, Brown, I am convinced of activity there!"

He groped under the table; in his excitement he had forgot to look for listening devices. Now he leaned forward and whispered, "Stringham was taken away yesterday. Three men came for him. As always. We must be careful, Brown; desperation is pushing them toward vengeance. Admiral Ironsides warned me in time; I left Cleveland only hours before Stringham was taken away."

"Who is Admiral Ironsides?" The name was new to me.

"He is retired. A good man; he is sponsoring my new research. Through old friends he was informed of what Intelligence was about to do." Santander began to eat; then paused, forkful of shredded carrots as if raised in tribute, and he said, "We are not likely to see Stringham again. I fear he has gone the way of Bohrod and the others."

"And now, perhaps, the general too," I said, watching his face.

He smiled. "No, Brown. The general is free. He spent the night at my house, in fact."

"Is he still there?"

"He left early this morning. Greystone is with him. Is the general sick?"

"Dying."

"Ah, one of those. A late riser, eh? As I thought. Ironsides is another. These men, so useless, can nevertheless be very useful, Brown. Have you noticed? One can employ their desperation like steam to drive the engine."

"It's dangerous, Santander. We may end up following them because there's no one else to lead, or because they are used to being followed. They command, and move off without even looking over their shoulders. One follows simply in order not to undermine so much confidence."

He shrugged. "They are useful to me. The admiral finances my research, and last night I got a letter of recommendation from your general. It will come in handy where I am going, a place where they still have respect for generals."

I looked at the cashier.

"I am soon leaving for Madrid," Santander said. "To look for the gold discs Montezuma gave to Cortez."

I turned back to him. "Surely they've been melted

down by now, Santander; five centuries of greed, they must have been found and spent by now."

"That fool Cortez! He called them *dishes!* Dishes! My God!"

"He could not have known; he was merely a soldier, a conqueror." Cortez wore that gritty deposit like armor, had a bellyful; it was a permanent itch, condition of his life. He died of it. Lesson to us all; which we will, of course, ignore.

"They were the discs they used to fly with!" Santander was going on, carrying on his argument not with me but with Cortez. "All the high nobility had them. It's in the records, clear for all to see now."

"Now, yes."

"Even then they should have seen it—a civilization so advanced, so far ahead of Europe—Cortez should have known there was some good reason why they did not have the wheel, a people like that, great astronomers, architects, mathematicians. If they did not have the wheel, it was not because they were incapable but because they did not *need* it!"

Cortez described the gold discs in his inventory of loot, the list sent to Isabella: one disc larger than the other, he noted. Of course; each was made in proportion to the size of the user. One belonged to Montezuma; the other to his queen. It is the only explanation of certain of the carvings. Flying chariots; men in air. They were the inheritors of Atlantis. What treasures lie buried in the layered depths below Mexico City; tourists walk there all unaware the future lies buried beneath their feet. They know no more than Cortez knew.

"There are museums in Spain, cellars full of stuff never examined or catalogued," Santander said. "They don't know what they've got. Who knows how much is there? I have rubbings of the carvings at Chichen Itza and Macchu Pichu and other places; I will know those discs when I see them. One of them *must* have survived, must have survived even these terrible centuries of ignorance. I will have aid. My nephew in Madrid is a Jesuit."

"In temperament, or actually?"

"Both."

"Most fortunate."

We drank our coffee. I watched her, the cashier.

"Yes," Santander said. He had noticed that I was looking at her. "Yes," he said.

"How long have you known?" I asked.

"Since the day she started working here."

Cunning of him to have recognized her. But it was her eyes; they made her origin unmistakable.

"Her name is Ethel Goren; her father works with me in the machine shop."

"What else?"

He shrugged. "A local girl." He smiled at that, the absurdity of it. I watched her; at that moment a pot was removed from the table next to the cash register and a cloud of steam haloed her head. "Her mother is dead," Santander said.

Clearly she was one of Them. We know They have placed some of Their people on earth: advance parties, studying our ways. They are among us. (Note: Tell of experience with Mary K.)

Santander rolled his paper napkin into a tight ball. "I must hurry back to the shop; there's a rush on for a new part."

"Don't tell me about it; I'd rather not know what you're up to here."

"We delay as much as we can, Brown."

"Are there many of you here?" I asked, surprised.

"I meant *we* in general; those like us. In any case, it takes only one to make a delay, Brown."

"Be careful, Santander."

He shrugged. Sadly, he said, "I wish I were close enough to something big that I had to worry about them. They're not about to take me in." Bitterly, he added, "They know I've got nothing to give them; nothing they can *use*."

I shook hands and wished him well. "I envy you, Santander," I said; and in a way this was true. Envied him not the grubby search but the thought of finding what he looked for; saw him in some museum's sub-basement dipping into a trunk of decaying mungy Indian woven stuff and, suddenly, his fingers strike the pure, hard object. Oh the thrill of ancient things, so well made, heartfelt, touched with mystery, graced by hairy gods and forgotten knowledge!

When he was gone I went back for a second cup of

coffee I did not want; I gave her a dollar so that I could stand there and look longer while she made change. She was not more than eighteen. She smiled. I thought again of Mary Kovarchuk. Back at the table I took out my wallet and looked for Mary's address. Perhaps I will send her a picture postcard from Arizona, I said to myself. Looking for her name I came across a list Greely and I had composed years ago: the people we suspected were not of this earth but sent here, the Selected Ones.

Here is the list:

Loretta Young.

Her sisters, the Blaine girls. (Where are they now? Have they gone back? Find out.)

Richard Nixon.

Laurel and Hardy.

The Bennett girls?—Doubtful.

Charles Lindbergh.

Max Beerbohm.

Ezra Pound.

Admiral Rickover?—Possible. Doubtful.

Frivolous, of course. But we were younger then, had joy, had not yet reached the barrier of desperation, the barrier of ultimate knowledge. We were not then aware of the possibility of exhaustion of creative powers, loss of the vital center. We did not know then that we are slowly being drained by Venus. It could mean the end of the West.

The coffee cup trembled in my hand; I turned and looked at her: she was smiling at me! Why had I looked in her direction then, at that moment? I thought of Galileo. "A sudden violent desire," he wrote, moved him and he turned his telescope on Jupiter, discovered the moons.

I left, went out to my car; averted, on the way, my eyes from the tapestry: that white hand. I drove toward the town and using another name (yet another!) I registered at a motel. Called myself Wainwright. Felt a satisfying sensation of slyness. Slept well. (Note: Tell of experience with Mary K.)

twenty

NEXT DAY, driving.

I should like to speak now about Mary Kovarchuk. Shall we stop here for a cautionary tale, something exemplary and illuminating to travel on? The continent is tipping, tilting; it flattens out and becomes paper on the car seat. Esso's cartographer has imposed his will; result: traveler's vertigo, often mistakenly called European tummy, Montezuma's revenge, etc., etc. Simple fear, rather; warranted, what's more. Think of the eyes of traveling salesmen. Recall Chichikov, that ringading-dinger and impulse buyer. It is the loneliness of man I'm thinking of; the breakages on the coasts of flesh; this sea of life enisled where myriad mortals live alone, eh, partner?

Let me admit it: I am a man of excessive desire, the result of extremes of loneliness—oh, such loneliness, like an abandoned broken fort—and like all such I quiver between lust and self-denial and give myself wholly first to one and then to the other, like a needle that knows no center and can register only Very Hot or Very Cold. Or perhaps it is (let me try to work this out before your very eyes), perhaps it is the letch for power that produces the excessive itch: well-known connection there: look at a Presidential candidate and you will see a well-blooded man, pincher and stroker, scourge of airline stewardesses, pursuer of secretaries and wives of best friends, a man who'd throw hat and *all* into the ring, kiss babies, *anything*. Yes, I should like to have it all in the palm of my hand, should like to have it all my way, am compulsive in my need to be right *and* President, central, the egg of all activity.

Meanwhile, however, meanwhile I played Prince Charming to Mary Kovarchuk the Sleeping Beauty, made my power-play, and left her fast asleep, the way I found her in the American teenager's cold stupor (our term for the dormant life of algae and lichen when kept in temperatures below freezing; oh yes, I know a thing or two).

She had a job in Personnel, ran personality-test papers through a machine and recorded results and made assignments. It had been worked out on a little wheel and was as sure as rain: Incipient Masturbator, recommend assignment to machine shop. Anal Erotic, assign to mathematician section. Paranoid, assign to security office. It is better to have a disease than to be unclassifiable, eh? God's mercy on them, the healthy unemployables. Mary must have got in by the skin of her teeth or, more likely, the shape of her breasts, not rated by any machine but by the personnel manager himself, a susceptible man, given to fantasizing, at bottom unfit for his job.

I made a date with her (not difficult in our careless society; life's a long holiday here for most), and gaitered, caped, ruffed, princely, charming, called for her where she lived with another girl, also employed yet unemployable, named Ruthie and very much of this earth, wholly unlike Mary who was clearly one of Them. Her aura was unmistakable and I trembled even seeing her through thicknesses of office-divider glass. I was afflicted by the same sickness of heart that touched me at sight of the girl in Santander's cafeteria. She is one too. Impossible to make contact. I know that now, but did not then that first night I called for Mary, thought then I was on the verge of touching the unknowable at last, thought I would soon (oh, I can move fast when I have to) embrace and be embraced by a perfect soul, one of those sent here to test and try us and see if our atmosphere is breathable. Of course these pilgrims have been washed clean of all memory of their world of origin, that perfect place; one day, their spell of duty among us over, they'll be recalled and, there, emptied of memories and experience of earth. It is all entered on punch-cards and will weigh heavily on their decision to come, or not to come, and aid us. Remember this, please, when you meet one of these perfect beings; show your best face; try to give the impression of being worthy.

Do we detect the bitterness of the jilted lover in that last remark?

Yes, friend, I think we do. Boys who give girls books to read are bound to lose. I won her and could have had her if I had been willing to have her as she was, but I was not and wanted to make her over or, to be precise, recall her to herself, wake her from the deep sleep and tap the knowledge within her. I began the first night, could not wait, had to have the power she could give me.

Meeting in autumn was bad beginning, I knew; oh the weather was fine enough but it's the season of despair and when it's that season, well, I despair. Autumn committed its pesty aggressions and so did I, but with half a heart; none at all, really, for when I put my hand under her skirt I wasn't foraging for love but for knowledge. Leaves meanwhile turned and fell and I was nowhere and ached like a boy. I had forgot how to court. Too many Stellas had spoiled me. I no longer knew how to neck and had to learn again. God's curse on little girls: I suffered the adolescent's aching back and began to examine the mirror for acne. I held hands in movies! I was told about *French* kisses and was warned there was a line could never be crossed; yes, like Richelieu she drew a holy circle round her hips and all that area became inviolate, not to be entered.

Villainous and cunning, I agreed and removed my hand at once, pretending a sadness that was genuinely felt. For reward she stroked my hair, that gentle, perfect, beautiful girl. I confess I left my maiming mark on her, yet do not fear she'll take back a bad report of me; she is too kind, she will protect me, I'm sure of it. My record's still clean with Them.

Mary Kovarchuk believed herself to be Polish, or Polish-American as she would say; she had no inkling of the clever stratagems that had placed her in the Kovarchuk cradle, was so simple a girl that she passed through childhood without once dreaming she had been born of royal blood, kidnaped by gypsies, sold to strangers. (Make you blush, does it? And are you absolutely certain you were wrong to have thought so?) She was blonde, blonde down to the core of her bones; her eyes are pure blue and have a marked oriental curve—result of Attila's invasion ho ho, ancestors sweeping down from the sack of Kiev. We know better. Possibly more the result of diet than heritage her body was Slavic, had suffered early maturing, but not excessively so; and this was more than made up for by the silicon perfection of her skin, waxy as certain fruits and as sweet. Oh the touch of her took my breath away and at the same time gave me strength; at first, in her embrace, I was powerful and helpless both, a strong man taxed to his limits, waiting for his second wind, but waiting in the wrong place. Her arms drained and sustained me, and she was all unaware of the one or the other, that sleeping beauty, victim of the cold stupor of our time and place. Pity, pity, pity.

Her house I need not describe: Greely's, but with no walls knocked down; she and her friend Ruth shared the second floor and used a common door with their landlady. It was one of those situations of complete trust, *tu sais*. She carried the baggage of family with her when she left home, the more fiercely perhaps because of her own first arrival, a beginner on Earth, trauma of her second birth. Entering the living room, one saw: the television. It dominated, all-seeing as much as seen. The sight of two girls living together always makes me sexually alert; my first thought on seeing Mary there, crouched, staring at the TV, was: I shall have her, and I shall have her in this very room. Melodramatic, if you like, but next time you talk to yourself, friend, please note how ornate your speech becomes. It's as if you were addressing a committee, isn't it?

Mary, suppliant before the box, reminded me of one of those members of a captive tribe being forced to adopt the god of her conquerors.

She was watching a program called Teeners' Bandstand. On the screen teenagers moved, dancing non-Cuban dances, boycotting the enemy. She, with her crystalline but blinded mind, watched.

Not until we got outside did she speak; then, seeing my car, she said, fantastically observant child: "I thought you'd have an Aston-Martin like all the other scientists." (I drive an old Plymouth because I like the ship riding ahead, vestigial radiator cap and bowsprit, and can imagine myself pushed by the wind rather than by the dirty engine under the dirty hood.)

In the car she sat close to me as I drove, turning the dial of the radio, picking up the local disc jockey. "I don't think you watch Teeners' Bandstand, do you, Bill?" she asked. "No, that's what I thought and that's why I ast you not to pick me up till eight o'clock. I never miss it. I want to go to New York and become a Teeners' Bandstand Regular."

But you can't! I cried to myself. Not when I have just found you, found you at last! Oh my darling, don't go, stay; I want to become a complete beginner with you.

"But I'm too old now," she said, downcast.

Thank God! (I did not know, you see, if I would ever find another, did not know then how frequently they appear among us.) I touched her: expression of sympathy.

"You're only eligible up to eighteen. After eighteen you have to leave the show. Rosa Posalippi had to leave last week after two years as a Regular. She got such marv presents from her fan club and her picture in *TV Screen Teenagers Guide* magazine. She's engaged to Rod Habib."

Her soul, I thought, her soul has lost completely the divine property of her first being. "Who is Rod Habib?" I asked, to show that I was listening.

"He's a Regular. Last year I wrote the editor of *TV Screen Teenagers Guide* magazine and ast how to become a Regular and it was printed and the editor said a lot of teeners ask how to become a Regular. Well, there's no way of answering that. All we can say is Regulars become Regulars because they're taken up by Regulars. Anat's true. You have to live in New York."

I will plunder you of everything, I thought; and the gold between your legs will be mine.

"You have to. If you don't, well, you'll never make it. Aneven if you do, you might not. There was this great boy Johnny Marschak who went there to New York and we all looked for him on Bandstand and waited and waited. But he never showed up."

"Has he come back?"

"No, Bill, it's jusas if he disappeared off the face of this earth. His parents haven't heard from him or anything. That's happened to a lot of kids and *TV Screen Teenagers Guide* magazine says Kids, don't go off to New York unless you have your parents' consent anenough money to tide you over."

Oh they're beginning to feel the pinch! They're beginning to feel it, to wonder what it's all about; people in back rooms trying to puzzle it out: children disappearing, setting off for New York, never heard from again. What does it all mean? they're asking themselves. We know of course that some day those children will return; some have already been sent back, transformed, crystal under the skin, another music remembered and reverberating in their heads. They are the ones—you've seen them—who never look lost, can stop smoking without a struggle, win Rhodes scholarships, never need glasses, can nap for twenty minutes and wake themselves, never have headaches, dream in full color, make love without sweating, shun all pills and laxatives, can drink coffee at night, never a cavity or ingrown toenail, can pick up an instrument and play without lessons, are never shortchanged or overcharged in supermarkets.

And the disc jockeys? those innocuous men with faces you can never quite remember, who wear black-rimmed glasses and speak without commas? I think not. I think it is the men behind them. They are the ones: they select these boy-men with unmemorable faces to play the Pied Piper for them; they stay out of camera range, are never interviewed, make no statements, live in Scarsdale, have memorable faces; they do not want to be seen. They are everywhere by now.

Mary wanted to see Troy Donahue's new movie. In Pittsburgh proper I put the car in a parking lot, and holding hands, we walked to the movie house. There were no seats; long lines of waiting boys and girls wound around the block and doubled back again. Vendors sold hot dogs and Cokes in paper cups. The air of that block hummed with energy, was charged with messages like old telephone poles. A thousand young and empty cold-stupor faces, there was not one Johnny Marschak among them, not one I saw who had a chance of being chosen; they were all Regulars, had accepted each other and everything else and never doubted we had won the War of 1812. Who is there to tell them?

We drove to a drive-in for hamburgers with french fries and Cokes. I thought Mary would be disappointed but she was not; she turned on the car radio and listened to Bobbie McSee, a local jockey whose real name was Bob McCaffery, a boy I had known in high school, doomed even then. She put her left arm along the back of the seat and, her head on my shoulder, sang along with Someone: I am sin-cere dear, I am sin-cere, since you have leffftme I've turned sin-cere.

"Oh, marv," she said. "Groovy!"

How perfectly she speaks our language, I thought, astonished by her will.

At the drive-in, after we had ordered, I told her how sorry I was we could not get in to see the film, and said, "Perhaps I can take you tomorrow. We could probably get in tomorrow if we got there earlier." (I was determined, even then, so early in the game, to wean her from Teeners' Bandstand.)

"It doesn't matter, Bill, but you are sweet." A drop of catsup fell on her chin; she scraped it off with her finger and sucked it clean, a charming gesture, wicked and innocent. "I've seen it twice already but it's so groovy, I mean it really swings, Bill, and I could see it again. I wanted to see it with you. Suzanne is in this really snobby school in Connecticut or somewhere . . ."

"Suzanne who?"

"Suzanne Pleshette. She plays opposite Troy. And she can't stand this snobby school so she goes to Rome and meets Rossano Brazzi who wants to romance her. Then she meets Troy. He's wearing this cute red sweater and has the bluest eyes—God, you should see them, Bill! Troy is going to an art school in Rome but, you know, his work isn't going well and he and his old girl friend can't make it any more. He and Suzanne get going at a café. They go away for a weekend to this really beautiful lake in Italy, and they pretend they're married. Her name in the movie is Prudence. She makes him sleep out on the terrace. Then they spend another weekend together; they go to the Alps mountains or some other mountains and they get very close but they still don't make it even though Troy says to her This time we'll be to-geth-er and you know he *looks* at her in that way. And then while they're there, up in the mountains, he says to Suzanne Excuse me for being profound at this moment but I realize what I've been missing. And you know he's thinking about his old girl who was so slick. Angie Dickinson. Then they're back in Rome and Suzanne gets to see Angie, the old girl friend, and Suzanne gets gished by it. It's at Angie's apartment and Suzanne is very polite and she says You have a lovely bedroom. You know, to be polite, but you can see it's making her want to vomit, the thought of Troy and Angie making it there. So she decides to go back to the USA. Then Angie makes a fool of Troy and he sees her for what she really is. He says My glasses were all fogged up. You know, realizing now. Then, you see Troy had this it looked like gold candelabra? And Suzanne said it was the symbol of his integrity? Then, at the end, at the railroad station and there's this great jam and Troy can't get to her but she sees the candelabra that he's holding up and she says to her parents There is my integrity!" Mary paused to sip her Coke. The drive-in's blue neon made ice of her face, betrayed her roots in silicon. "You're a quiet one, aren't you," she said.

I drove her to my apartment. "There's a tape I want you to hear," I said. Cunning, yes, but when I unlocked the door my hand was trembling, for I had at that moment prevision of unlocking her and emptying her like a chest of her jewel-secrets. I'd decode her tumblers with my pirate fingers or pry her open, if need be, with my fingernails, jimmies, ball-peen hammers.

She kicked off her shoes and, taking a pillow from the sofa, lay down on the floor. "How many speakers have you got, Bill?"

"Two, I think. It came that way."

"Oh," she said.

"This," I said, threading the tape, turning switches, "this is a recording made at the radio-telescope observatory in Arizona." Hissing; then sounds began, voices so fantastically enlarged they had lost all humanity. Another way must be found.

"Do you have the one with the train whistles, Bill?"

"These are radio signals picked up from far space," I explained, and watched her eyes all the while. "Radio telescopes can pick up waves even from underdeveloped hydrogen atoms existing in almost empty space."

"What they won't think of," she said; and I was pleased to see she had a sense of wonder.

The cracklings were finished and now came the gleeps, grawps, craangs. She listened. Celestial voices filled the room: gloop, gleep, graw, mang, farng, smung; whispers; roar and growl of that fabulous ocean, scrambled beyond understanding. She looked back at me; perfect eyes. I touched her hand. "You can undo my bra if you want to, Bill, but that's as far as I go. I'm a serious girl." I put my hand under her blue sweater. The light was out. In the darkness her skin became luminous. Even in my shadow she glowed, silver, lunar. Smarm, sneep, blop, koop, meem, lum, sang, jahm jahm, hoom hoop mens uhm: the tape span through, she made no sign, how cunning they are. Perfect teenager, I thought, my hands discovering her; perfect and unflawed by memory of the higher sphere she was born to or disgust at her role; not made sick by hamburgers, popcorn, Cokes; oh perfect, perfect. She even smelled Polish.

Like certain saints she was too perfect to be helpful; I know it now. Like Teresa she would scold even God. Besides, her function on earth precluded her helping me; I know that now. Or to put it more accurately: *it was made known to me*. Such insights come always from elsewhere. Even so, but even so, in our desperation we go on trying; I had hoped she'd be the Rosetta Stone that would unlock for me the glawps and gleeps—they're trying to tell us something!—of those celestial voices. In a sealed-off part of her, in some blocked and sealed-off chamber she holds her secrets like the body of a pharaoh, wrapped in gold like a nougat. There she holds the knowledge of that language, and of more, of so much more. Of all.

No, she was too perfect. Even her odor, that nose-clogging air of a Polish kitchen, it might have been made in a lab, so right it was. (And it probably was; a simple matter; any organic chemist can duplicate it.)

I saw her every night of the week but one, that night being, of course, the night of Stella's therapeutic visit. At the same time (I'm a fair man) I tried to force *and* arm her, struggled to pirate her gold and yet provide her with defenses: gave her books to read, took her (once) to the art museum. She liked the Impressionists. "They sure are pretty, Bill dear." I wanted her, you see, to go back to Them with a few small gems mined by us here on earth, hoping that way They'd not think us completely lost and unreclaimable, would find us worthy of saving. I gave her Homer to read and Sophocles, Shakespeare, Baudelaire, *Notes from the Underground* and *Dead Souls,* Flaubert, Turgenev, Céline, as well as selected poems by my favorite English and German poets.

She never read them. She never read them. Could not. Our schools had spoiled her for literature. I could not test her, could I? Did not wish to show myself as a suspicious man. But I am certain she never read them. Whenever I gave her a new one, a look of absolute anguish came over her face; and when she returned a book and I'd say, for example, "Wasn't it fine?" she'd say, "I liked that part where he goes to Africa." I always knew that was the only part she had read, always a few pages so that she could say, "I liked that part where he went to Africa." Or, "That one about the angels was beautiful, Bill dear." But perhaps some of it, in spite of all, got through; and when They purge her of earthly memories, there among the mess of old hamburgers will be one line of Rilke.

But if I pursued, if I said, "Yes, and what about Robinson, a fantastic character, eh?"—then she would never know what to say and say, "Oh Bill," her voice full of tremulous Hollywood yearning, all learned from B-films, that most widely used visual aid of our young. To stop my mouth she'd put her tongue in it: French kiss, *tu sais,* friend. Well, it was like the tiger coming to the altar; if it comes often enough, you make it part of the ritual. So I did; and when I wanted her I had only to begin talking about a book. High and dry in her cold stupor all she could do was embrace me, kiss and grapple.

Not content, never content with less than all, I came in time (soon enough) to use the threat of cultural uplift as a wedge for entering that holy circle around her hips, where the gold is. I let her feel the weight of my adulthood, a not-to-be-underestimated weapon in wooing a young girl. I used hands, knees, tongue, tampered with everything until she could breathe only through her mouth and promise to faint. In a week we lay completely naked on the floor, listening to the radio-telescope tapes. How many nights my hands sought pasture on her and my tongue drubbed her nipples while we listened to the crangs and graws and gleeks. Were they, I have since often wondered, were they parental voices warning her against me? Old friends telling her to hold fast against the uncircumcised dog? *Did she understand those voices?* As we will see, she did indeed.

I made demands, which made her cry, which broke my heart; and I promised always never to make them again. I made them again. I said, "Darling, I cannot help myself. This thing is stronger than I am." Language she understood.

On the tenth night, when I told her I had bought tickets for the symphony (to provide her with a bit of Beethoven and Bartók to take home with her, some beauty in the baggage of mung), she undressed at once and without any urging, stripped down to her perfect luminous skin. And not the floor this time. I got her onto, if not into, the bed; a great advance on floors, I'm here to say.

"But won't we be late for the show, Bill?"

"Concert," I said, an educative force to the very end.

"Concert, Bill; we'll be late, darling." This last she crooned like Suzanne Pleshette or, I don't know, Angie Dickinson.

"Do what I ask and we may not go at all, dearest." I tried to sound like Troy Donahue, difficult since I had never heard him speak, but willed myself young, blue-eyed, clean-limbed. In my ears it sounded more like George Raft—a star she could not know—sinister and tough, yet willing to be loved.

"Won't it hurt you, dear?" she asked, her eyebrows drawn together, already feeling *my* pain.

"Not if you're careful," I said. And I caressed her while she had my way with me (oh the things that go on in bedrooms!); later, dried her tears, gave her coffee, played Our Tape: crang woop! How jubilant the voices were that night; yet not, of course, victorious. God alone knows what they really said. When the voice, at the tape's halfway point, roared *Yahn roop hawn,* she turned on me her perfect eyes, lashes till glistering, and said, "I love you, dear, more than I can say, anat's sincere, Bill."

I could not see her the next night because of Stella; I feared the pursuit of Mary Kovarchuk might lose momentum, yet could not—could I?—deny Stella her opportunity for displacing energy. Stella and I are joined together by science and obsessions, which perhaps comes to the same thing. (One feels not so much a *call* to science, as a compulsion.) Stella complained that night of a falling-off of ardor on my part. I denied it. It was true. My thoughts were elsewhere. I thought only of Mary and Stella's body seemed at once both meagre and gross, as if her bony thinness were the result of avarice. Stella is not for savoring, she is merely a product—like all the rest; that is to say, disposable. Conceived perhaps by the Master but molded, surely, by lesser hands. I say "perhaps," but—why not face this?—God's work may have stopped aeons from where we now stand. We are, I believe, a spontaneous and makeshift product; so much in our construction uninspired and gimcrack; we are undone by built-in obsolescence. We die. The Others are immortal. They were conceived with forethought, are the result of planning, experiment, divine effort. We, on the other hand (meaningful phrase), are the grudged products of celestial necessity, here for one reason only: to give Them reason for being there. They, perfect beings, were created to save us, to save us from ourselves.—Please underline this last passage. Put a check mark in the margin. Turn down the corner of the page. One day, and it is not so far off, you'll see the truth of this and will want to find this message and read it again. You will say, "Oh, why did I not take it to heart *then!*" I only hope, when such time comes, that it will not be too late for you, friend.

On the next night, when I called for Mary at her house, I found her for the first time alone, her roommate gone. Mary sat on the hard maroon sofa, she was crying, the TV's dead eye stared at her, gone silver with grief. "I thought you weren't going to come, Bill. I thought you mighta lost respect for me."

I fell on my knees. I protested. I embraced and consoled and picked at the buttons of her blouse. Tears had softened her, swollen her face; words like *membranes* and *ducts* sprang to my mind. I smelled gold. Imaginary earring biting my right lobe, piratical, fingertips numb with excessive desire, I caught her with grappling hooks, swung her round, boarded and pillaged her yo ho ho, sacked hold and keep, heard keel scrape on the maroon rock. Sank her. Divine being. Oh the delight to have entered her silicon essence, pushed aside immortal membrane, penetrated chamber where Pharaoh sleeps, and embraced at last (I thought), and was wholly embraced by, this precious being full of knowledge. Oh, what homecoming! My hands, all, sensitive now as seismographs, registered her every tremor and vibration. She hummed liked telephone wires, like Amer-Russe nights, like hydrogen atoms in far space: messages to be read. I shall decode them later, I told myself, a hard promise, blood vow. I listened, held her in my hands like a shell, brought her to my ear and heard the conch-roar of vast distance.

"Let's go have some hamburgers, dear," she said.

La Divina was hungry for chopped meat! (Oh how he is bitter, bit-ter!)

I took her to the drive-in, Our Place, *tu sais*. Was happy that night. Felt power in my wrists. Knew myself to be on the very edge of discovery. Thought of

Lord Rutherford; saw myself ennobled by grateful world. How vain. Yet irresistible, these thoughts, eh? What American boy has never dreamed of being King of England? Damned few.

But I was not content for long. Three exquisite nights with Mary (an actor-out of fantasies, wanton, abandoned; well, yes, or course, abandoned) left me just where I had been. I had the gold, yes, but found it bought me nothing, was not negotiable in her world. I smelled of rubber; wanted to cut her open like a melon and pick the seeds of knowledge from her crystal brain and plant those splinters in my own; knew the shoots would root there and, this way, I'd become one of Them, a citizen by aggression. I don't care. I'd shoot my way in if I had to.

Perverse to the point of imbalance in bed—and with a drum-majorette's athletic vigor, as well; often I half expected her, at certain points, to begin to chant a Pittsburgh High School locomotive—outside of it she was innocent of everything and balanced to the point of absolute inertia. (Oh They had done a good job on her!) A fertile lack of balance is what's wanted, what I, in fact, have found and you, dear friend, still seek. Well, stick around; given this region where we live and breathe it will descend on you, soon, like God's grace. By means mechanical or psychological they had taken it all out of Mary. Did I call her perverse? Nonsense. It must seem so to you and me but, in fact, she was simply natural, the way all women must surely be in that land. Sainthood, you will remember, can be achieved by asceticism *or* a total indulgence of self. It is clear that we must choose the second way. In this matter of the bed, my dear, we have got to go ahead and become beginners.

But before discontent set in, what days and nights of intoxication; the height of it all being that night—early morning, rather—when, exacerbated almost beyond bearing by desire and repletion, I heard Mary in her abandonment (no better word!) cry out in a strange language. Later, when I questioned her, she said, "It was prolly Polish. My parents are Polish-American, Bill, an I prolly picked it up from them."

Was she being sly? Did she really believe it? Was it, in fact, Polish? Later I could not remember the words, was never able to find out. But when she spoke them, there, on the bed, in that fabulous lunar light, the blood froze in me and I had such a fear as I had never known before, the kind of fear a man knows only when he steps forward into regions of the wholly unfamiliar, into worlds where sky and earth can change places and functions and we are all suns.

She would not be broken. I could wrest nothing from her but B-film love, acquiescence to any sexual scheme, and a fantastic energy in the pursuit thereof. With these she was generous to a fault. Words like *membrane* were no longer in my mind; instead, I thought of such words as: *knife, wedge, can opener, crowbar, catheter, faucet, funnel, bottle.* I dreamed only of tapping those incredibly rich deposits; compared to me the diamond-rich of Johannesburg and the oil men of Texas would be as nothing. I could buy and sell them. No Faust, mind you! None of your German pandering for yours truly! I'd not sell or give up anything, I'll make no deals but take what I want and give no quarter. I bore down.

I gave up the threat of culture. I withdrew sex. I stayed away from her door for two days but on the second night, late, she came knocking on mine, tearful, soft with surrender. Impossible to resist. She stayed the night and fixed me breakfast. I toyed with the idea of marriage. Perhaps, having the confidence the marital bed is said to give, she'd answer my questions, tell all. But later, in my office, I slapped the desk like a hotshot executive and said, "No! By God we'll do this *my* way!" Whatever that may have meant. Posturing. Whenever we're alone, we posture. (Conducted any good orchestras lately, friend?)

That night I put on the tape and took her (metaphorically) by the throat. "Tell me," I hissed in her ear, "tell me, damn you, tell me what they're saying!"

"Honey, I don't know what they're saying," she said.

"Don't lie to me, liar. Liar! Liar! *Tell me!*"

"You're scaring me, Billy dear. How shouldeye know what they're saying?"

"You know!"

"I *don't* know!"

"Listen to it!"

"I *am* listening."

"Just listen and shut up!"

"Oh, Bill dear . . ."

"Listen!"

"You're hurting my arm, Bill . . ."

She began to cry. Naturally, I calmed her, stroked her hair, apologized. "Listen to me, Mary," I said, my voice fatherly and just, "you don't know it but you are something special."

She smiled. "No, I'm not. Oh, Bill, I'm jussa local girl."

"You are very special, Mary . . ."

"You are sweet, Bill."

". . . and you know a great deal more than you think you know." My voice was soft, soothing, I repeated every phrase. The idea of hypnosis came to me; I wondered how long it would take me to learn it. I recalled an old story by Rudyard Kipling (no favorite of mine!) in which a man is made to lose himself by looking deep and long into a puddle of ink. "There is so much you could tell me, Mary. So much. If only you would!"

"Honestly, Bill darling, I'd tell you *en*-ny-thing. But I don't know ennything, honestly. I love you, Bill."

"Then tell me."

"I love you."

She brought magazines of a certain sort to my apartment; she showed me full-color, full-page advertisements for silverware. "Which pattern do you like best, Bill," she asked, "this one called Forever or this one called Bliss?"

"Bliss," I said, because the knives of Bliss had sharper points.

One night I put a puddle of ink under her nose and she screamed.

We were both tired.

A few nights later, after she had said "Bill, I love you an I'd do ennything for you but I don't *know* ennything, honest" for the thirtieth time, I slapped her in the mouth. I was made desperate by frustration. Besides, like every other man, I have always wanted to hit a woman. I mean really *hit* one, you know. She ran away. I phoned, often, but all her roommate would say was, "She doesn't wanta talk to you, you rat!" I drove to Mary's house every night, parked, and watched her door for hours; she never came out. I wrote letters, long ones; I bared my soul and, in order not to frighten her, quoted no one. It embarrasses me to think those letters might yet be read by others. Still. I continued phoning, of course; and finally, after two weeks of fear and desperation and, yes, longing, *she* answered the phone, heard my voice, burst into tears. I ran to her arms, promised everything, the maroon sofa received us. I proposed. She accepted. At last! I would be the son-in-law of Someone!

But in joy I fumble. After all, it is an exotic condition, eh? We don't know how to handle it. I tried to be gentle. I used hypnosis. Mary cooperated. I told her that learning it was essential to my job and she wanted to take an interest in my ho ho work. Copies of a magazine called (really, I sometimes wonder how I ever got into such a situation) *Brides' Monthly* lay in her lap, waiting to be consumed; she put them aside in order to help me; she was taking an interest in my work; it made her cheeks glow with vigor. I had been studying a book on hypnosis, in preparation for this: to no avail. I could not even induce her to close her eyes. "Close your eyes," I said, and spoke without exclamation points, my voice calm, drowsy, decaffeinated. "Relax, relax, relax."

"I am relaxt, dear."

And she was, she was; it was the total, nothing held back relaxation of cold stupor; there was not a thought in her head to put her on edge, keep her awake. Once I asked her what she thought about when she thought about death. "I never think about it, Bill," she said. I insisted she think about it; I gave her a minute or two to mull it around; then asked again. "Well?" "Well, Bill, I think it is just like falling asleep."

Hypnosis failed. Even the pleasures of the bed began to deteriorate. Mary never had much to say at the best of times; and I, now, had sealed my lips with my own promises. She lay in bed, on her belly, and read *House Beautiful*. I gazed at her butt, overwhelmed by effort and satiety, felt myself falling into that teenager boredom so deep that the victim can never recover.

"Do you like split-levels or ranch, Bill dear?"

For a whole day (I admit it) I doubted she was one of Them, thought I had made a terrible mistake; ratcheted from pole to pole, believing, doubting, convinced, uncertain. That night I watched her every move, read deeply into every utterance. Nothing. Our engagement had been announced—she wanted a short one, she said—I had broken it off with Stella—and now I called myself all kinds of fool. How would I ever get out of it? Saw myself throwing up job and all and moving to another town. But then she turned off the lights, put on Our Tape, and curled up in my arms. I put my right hand on her perfect breast and in the middle of the tape felt her heart lurch—*hoom hawp eem,* and her heart lurched and raced. "What is it?" I said, and moved to see her face. "Nothing, dear," she answered. I could hear the breath whistling in my nostrils, blood's taffeta rustle in my temples; I practised cunning. I pretended to look away but out the corner of my eye watched her face and I saw, as she listened, the look of ineffable cunning in her eyes and around her mouth a smile flickered, arrogant, lewd with secrets.

I pulled her to her feet. "You know! You know!" I cried through clenched teeth. "You know and will not tell me, me who loves you!"

Her mouth had fallen open; she looked at me with disbelief as I raised my hand and struck her face. I hit her several times, in fact. She fell and, in raising her up, I ripped her dress, helping her. Holding the torn panels together she ran to the door, crying. Fury rooted me. I did not chase her but picked up books from the coffee table and flung them at her; while she struggled with the locks I flung them at her—Baudelaire, Céline, Flaubert; paperbacks, mostly, but a few in hard covers—some missing, many striking her back and head. The tape's idiot voices cranged, heeped, hooed; door slammed; I was left alone in the darkened room with one last book in my hand. I threw it at the door.

Phone calls. More letters. The phone again. I was in despair, thought I had lost my one great chance for entry into that world, those celestial corridors of power. No response. Ruthie, her roommate, finally came to feel sorry for me. One night, as I was sitting in my car in front of their house listening to Bobbie McSee, Ruthie came out and talked to me. "I know how you feel, Bill. But it's all over an finished with you two an you gotta forget about her. I hate to haveta tell you this, Bill, but Mary says if you go on hanging around like this she is going to haveta call the police." I said nothing. She handed me an envelope and went away.

I drove home before reading the letter, the only letter Mary ever wrote me; I suspect it may be the only letter she has ever written, if we do not count the one to the editor of *TV Screen Teenagers Guide*. Here (I don't care) is the letter:

Dear Bill;
Ill never love another the way I loved you Bill and that is sinceer. But its all over Bill and thats all I can say. Youre a swell person Bill and Ill always think of you as a real friend in time of need.
Yours truly,
Mary Kovarchuk.

She quit her job in Personnel soon after, perhaps because she saw me hanging around there, several times a day, for a sight of her. I could smell her right through the cinder-block walls. After a week I ceased thinking of suicide. What do we really know about it? I started going to see Greely again. But still I dreamed of Mary, her body and embrace, the sweetness of her thighs. After two weeks I phoned Stella and told her I was free again.

"Well, Billy," she said, "the fact is, I'm booked up solid right now."

I let my silence express the disappointment I felt.

She said, "Well Christ, Billy, how many guys can a girl ball in one week?"

She called a few days later to say that she could fit me in, poor questing girl; and as my attentive reader in Urduland knows, I have been with her ever since, a service station on her road to freedom.

It was about six months after this that I read of Mary's marriage; a local boy, a machinist or mechanic of some kind. I saw her once, coming out of a department store. She was pregnant. She lowered her eyes when she saw me. Not surprising, is it? She knew she had betrayed me.

Now, driving away from Wabash, early in the morning, a day behind the general, I think of her again, the poor brainwashed child. Back home again They'll have to scrub her clean of every memory, of our schools, schooling, TV, movies, comic books, potato chips, corn flakes, catsup. What a gigantic purging it will have to be. Some danger in it, I suppose, for Mary. Suppose they do not wholly succeed and, in dreams perhaps, she is visited by a half-purged vision of Troy Donahue, a fragment of American history, some piece of weighty ignorance left over from Social Studies or Current Events; or walking one day across that fabled plaza be reminded that we won the War of 1812, or suddenly hear the language of comic books reverberating in her perfect brain: wham, pow, sock, !!!!!, ?????, zinggggg, screeeech, yow, gulp. Or, lying on some fantastic beach there, head full of sun, eyes closed, hear tags and pieces of disc-jockey music. Will she not sit up, startled, a little frightened, and look around to see where is it coming from? Then sit there, wondering what does it all mean, frightened as we are frightened by the fragment of a memory of a bad dream.

Or suppose they forget and leave her here to live out her life in ignorance and die all unaware? It's possible; a simple error in accounting, a tiny flaw in a great machine so perfect its imperfections are never discovered. It could happen. Ah, the horror of it. But I won't think of it or consider that possibility any longer; too frightful; the hollow voices of exiles; worst fate of all, never quite touching, reality slipping away, caught in the toils of another language, *at a loss for words!*

No!

But I wonder how they will empty her, how erase memory, scars, nostalgia, remove all marks of the hooded disguise, agonies of alienations, the terrifying removes, bracken of impulse and responses? And when they've removed it all, what do they do with it? The poisons of chopped meat, white bread, adulterants, vaccines, Rice Krispies. Put it all in lead containers, I suppose, and sink them somewhere in far space, an elliptic (God's perfect circle is an ellipse) moving monument to us, eternal reminder of our mistaken ways. It may be all that's left of us when we break this world like a walnut, shell and meat, obliterate the sweetness in one great pow, boing, wham; and there we'll be, all that remains of us the dredgings of the mind of a teenage girl: gossip of movie stars, songs of Presley, the *Gleaners* of Millet, the *Mona Lisa,* Ravel's *Bolero,* Sing Along with Mitch, Champagne Music of Lawrence Welk, a short speech from *Romeo and Juliet,* the first line of a Wordsworth poem: I wandered lonely as a cloud. Also: shardlike memories of Scrooge, the murmuring pines and the hemlocks, the pledge of allegiance, national anthem, middle Atlantic States, odor of chalk and wet blackboards, the sound of a Princess telephone, theme music of the Late Late Show, alarm clock buzz, doodled textbook covers, Band-Aids, mittens, a scotch plaid thermos. And Alfred Hitchcock Presents. And that's about all.

Whizzzz, boing, pow! There we are.

fourth proclamation

¶ For every finite quantity of matter there is a finite quantity of unique euents. ¶ The world is, therefore, a sequence of events that cannot be repeated. ¶ When it goes, it goes for good.

twenty-one

FOR TWO DAYS I drove, yoked to map, and covered the deadlands (well named, friend), trying to catch up with the general. A marine voyage: all this land was once under water. Lemuria was the first to go. Its memorials are everywhere: dinosaurs in tar pits; monster hoof and claw prints in the soft rocks, preserved by time, fossil souvenirs of an age of desperate yearning when man fumbled to find the perfect form, and failed. Morning now, and thinking of the sadness of *places* I arrived at last in Wunter, hoping here I'd find the general.

I was following Oliver's list, letting it guide me as a map guides; I moved across the continent on that underground railroad of our time, handed from hand to hand, from yearner to seeker to would-be discoverer, from one wheelerdealer of the soul to another. A line without brakemen and with green lights only—oh we'll go charging through, friend, don't you worry, just you wait; Casey Joneses and eighty-cars chockablock with will, daring every hairpin along the way, coupling, uncoupling, tapping hotboxes at dawn on lonely sidings.

Tired. Need I tell you? I was tired. Memory of Mary exhausts my fire. She sleeps in me. Every wind charges her to flame, ignites, depletes me. Well, never mind, think how close I was. I touched it! At least I touched it; which puts me one up on you, friend, puts me way out and far ahead, breathless perhaps but more likely to break the tape (feel its grace across my chest) than you, what? I am become material for myth: sojourner in other-world, mingler with the only true foreigners—man who has truly made the Grand Tour, an Orpheus without the faggy appeal. You hear?

Hoped here in Wunter I'd find the general. He had been and gone; on the porch of the Dana home I found only his tracks. Mrs. Dana at the door, a name on Oliver's list come to life, trappings of flesh. Her face still glowed with the pride of having had him. She said, "Such a distinguished guest." She simpered, something I had never seen before but knew it at once for what it was. "Such a fine man. So inspiring." She touched her hair.

The mother of a prodigy, Mrs. Dana moved as such people always move: with the knowledge that they're being watched, that people are always ready to talk; she knew she had to be twice as good as anybody else. In Wunter, goodness is gentility; saints simper and always take *small bites.*

Mary Jane Dana, her daughter, was not yet home. A registered nurse by trade, a seer by divine dispensation, Mary Jane (her mother informed me) was working the night shift with a dying lady and would not be home until ten. She invited me in, insisted on breakfast. "Won't you have flapjacks, Mr. Brown?"

"Only coffee," I said.

Smiling small, she said, "I'm famous in Wunter for my flapjacks."

In a house of women, as always, I felt manly and accepted her offer: *flapjacks,* such a virile word. I watched her move toward the kitchen, slick and reptilian in her elasticized slacks and cotton T-shirt. Her head belonged to another body. Or possibly not. Possibly her body had all her life been on a long holiday of hikes and volleyball, and only her head had worried itself into age and took no toll below the neck. Or: born lucky, as she would have said.

The living room contained what is called a suite of furniture: rose plus, and seldom seen outside the windows of small-town furniture stores. A full-color reproduction of Custer's Last Stand hung over the empty fireplace; evil Indians and valiant whites locked in combat; the best man ho ho lost. A Dana had died there, she said. And it had happened not so many miles away, that fantastic event. I looked out at the flatlands stretching away to the rim of earth. When They come, I thought, here one will be able to see Them coming a long way off.

I would like to live in a sod house, odor of earth always in my nostrils. That way I'd not be able to forget for a moment how basely born I am.

I would like to have been born in frontier times and abducted by the Sioux or the Comanches and raised as one of them, guided by dreams, the bearer of a secret name. Speak it aloud and I die! Smelling of hides, eating roast dog with a knife, buying a wife when the fancy struck me.

I would like to live without the numbing knowledge of my time and place. I'd rather (really) never have learned about the electric circuit and aperiodic crystals. I'd prefer to be simple and unresistant, capable of being swept away—devoured even—by the wind of a great idea.

Then, when the messenger comes knocking at my door, I'd be like those who say "Come in and welcome"; and not: "Who are you?"

I am taken with the notion of simple strength; I would like to taste the scented wine of noble brutes.

I desire to have been brought up among those who hallow and praise all things; who see in a flower only beauty and not (Darwin's words) an abominable mystery.

But what's desired is not always to be achieved; and I find it quite impossible as you, my friend, to bypass the dirty machine—simply pass it by without a glance or a thought. Impossible. I am as lost as Mrs. Dana in her Maidenform bra. I am blasted, deformed and trivialized by learning; knowledge has pierced me, left me with the center paralyzed, and now feeds off me—supplier and parasite both, ugly parent giving and taking with the same hand.

Waiting for the flapjacks I must have dozed. Woke to find this message lying beside the conch shell on the table next to me:

Dear Mr. William Brown
Distinguished Sir:
In the golden light of my yak oil lamp I take pen

in hand. Why do I write you, sir? What is all this reaching out in aid of (as my Anglo-Indian schoolmaster would say)? It is loneliness, Mr. William Brown—"this sea of life enisled," etc., as one of our former imperial masters wrote—because of this it is that I extend my hand. It is the lonely condition of man causes me to seek others like myself.

Odd—is it not?—you should find me here in this remote place, your so utterly different double: I am, after all, a boy who gourmandizes on rancid butter, who lives in the Himalayan shadows, in a country with dubious boundaries; you, on the other hand, are repelled by rancid butter, know not what it is to be landlocked, have forgot the thrill of fire, are now in Wunter—pop. 964. Distinguished Sir, loneliness makes us kin. Both of us are aware of "signs and rumours of some knowable kindred beyond." (John Livingston Lowes.) Underdeveloped people are forever quoting developed people; but perhaps you have already noticed this. Ah my dear friend, knowable kindred, fellow creature—can we not ignore national differences? Are we not both God's spies? (Oil running low in the lamp now.) Time for a final word: Let us all begin to keep a diary like your Miss Anne Frank; for any night or day now it will come, that KNOCK.

Your Reader in Urduland.

Mrs. Dana entered; china tinkled and warned of her coming. On the tray were the famous flapjacks, and above them, on guard and menacing as cannon, her conical breasts. They kept watch. They looked like something built up slowly over many years by industrious ants. Faugh!

"Tuck in," she said. "I like to see a man eat. The general, I must say, is not a good eater."

"He is not well." Eating flapjacks now, I squared my shoulders, imagined myself burly in a lumberjacket and with jaw muscles that bulged, ropy and oiled, as I ate.

"I could see he needed a tonic." She stroked the second skin of her slacks; and raised her needle-thin eyebrows as if opening her face for inspection. Clearly this woman thought herself to be the tonic the general needed. "He is the kind of man people will follow, Mr. Brown.

He puts me in mind of General Custer, who happened to be a personal friend of my great-grandfather. The general had only to beckon and men followed him. A man like that does not often appear on the scene, Mr. Brown. One every generation, maybe two at the most." Her old-lady head was serious, concerned, and cracked with lines she had no right to; her girl-body, easy in the rosy chair, was lithe and slick. Something mythic about this woman, I thought; any moment now she will lean forward, body braced between her clawed hands, and ask me a riddle. And after all, she *is* the mother of her daughter, that astonishing girl; she had carried within her that being who contains the fabulous secrets of Atlantis.

Mrs. Dana stood up to pour me more coffee; then, hands on hips, looked out the window at Wunter before sitting down again. "Well, Mr. Brown, weren't those flapjacks everything I said?"

The best I had ever eaten, I said. Oh, I can be gracious too. (To what depths of gentility the word *grace* has fallen! Oh God how it has come down in the world! Soon they'll be breaking it up into Studio Apts. five to a floor; they'll put in Hollywood beds and recessed kitchens. That will be the end. While-U-Wait service-stores on the ground floor, of course. Please make a note of this.)

Back ramrod straight as her ancestor's she looked again out the window, at Main Street, the storefronts machine-made in some sinister suburb of Detroit, in a factory dedicated to ugliness and the depredation of the American landscape, a factory owned by a man who is *devoted* to his family. Find that man! Seek him out, run him to ground! Look for the give-away stain of plastics on his right hand, the madness of Disneyland aesthetics in his eye! Catch him! He is subversive! He would bury us!

"Wunter is a progressive, go-ahead town, Mr. Brown. We are doing things to attract industry. The town fathers have plans."

"What have they done thus far, Mrs. Dana?"

"They have chopped down all the trees along Main Street. We think it looks more businesslike that way."

Silence in the room then; saturation point has been reached; shock, then stillness. Equilibrium becomes a chemistry textbook diagram in my head. Note how I am still afflicted by the need to make mystery literal and visible. (Note to myself: *Work on this!*)

Mrs. Dana looked at her watch. "Mary Jane will be home soon," she said, and sighed. "I'm lucky, Mr. Brown. She is a sweet, normal girl and hard-working and level-headed, in spite of her great gifts. It could have been much, much worse. I often think of that German girl I read about years ago in Robert Ripley's *Believe It Or Not*, poor thing."

"Which German girl was that?"

"She had holes in her hands—one in each hand—and on Good Friday blood oozed out. I often think of that girl's mother and what she had to put up with. *That* girl spent most of her life in bed." She shook her head, full of sympathy, a mother's understanding crossing national boundaries. "All those people flocking in once a year, all at one time, on Good Friday, to have a look." Visions of muddy boots on new-scrubbed floors undid her; eyes bugged. "When I think of the *sheets* that woman must have had to change in her lifetime! How she must have *dreaded* Good Friday!" She stretched her cobra neck and looked out the window for sign of her daughter. "Mary Jane has been a credit to me. Not high-strung, not delicate, she has taken her great gifts in stride. She goes into trance as easy as pie and don't make a big deal of it, I'll tell you. Not like some others I could name, Mr. Brown—I'm sure you know who I mean—who make such a fuss and conditions have to be just so and *then,* when they finally get into trance, you got to go tippy-toeing around and hardly breathing. Why, I've seen Mary Jane—two years ago, for example, at the convention in California—there were forty photographers must have been, popping flashbulbs right under her nose, and it didn't disturb her at all. Not one bit. She stayed in trance, as solid as this chair I'm sitting on, reporting her Atlantean testimony, telling about the monstrosities and the depraveds and all that. I guess you read the book they wrote about her?"

Mary Jane's Chevrolet pulled up to the curb. I watched; she parked it expertly, obviously very much at home with the things of this world. (I hear you ask: Why was Mary Jane Dana chosen as a vessel? The answer is a simple one: In mystery is the true democracy. In that strange territory angels seek out shepherds, Mary makes herself visible to shoeless Portuguese children, saints to lepers. Have you ever been kissed by Ev Dirksen? Has Hubert

Humphrey ever raised anyone from the dead? Who *are* those people down in Washington that we should place our lives in their care? Remember that at Antioch St. Andrew confided the great news to a poor peasant; "God has chosen you poor folk from amongst all people," St. Andrew said. So it goes. They are, I believe, the hidden, final, holy people.) Mary Jane parked her car where no tree was; or, rather, where tree was and no tree is. Town fathers will kill us surely, leaving us without a stick of shade to preserve us on the great plains; us, clamped between the bracketing horizons. Oh we could die of it, friend, we could die of it.

Mrs. Dana opened the door and we watched Mary Jane come up the walk, the white uniform over her arm like the train of a ball gown. She wore black slacks and a red jersey. Her hair, straight, was cut short and sat on her head like an antique freshman beanie.

"How is she?" Mrs. Dana wanted to know, asking after the patient.

Mary Jane shrugged her broad shoulders. "She'll be dead by four o'clock."

"God bless her soul," Mrs. Dana said, and shivered with feeling. "Mary Jane, meet Mr. William Brown, a friend of the general."

An ordinary girl when not in trance and guided by those perfect hands; the memory of others gives her importance. She is peopled by beauty, thronged by mystery but, awake, she is a registered nurse, nothing more; a lost soul, like the rest of us. Trance or hypnosis transforms her, carries her up beyond the surface of the daily to a high consciousness; danger of vertigo on those peaks for the rest of us; the mortal nosebleed. Then that unremarkable mouth opens and words issue forth that must once have been written on illuminated parchments: breathings of bird-souls, constructs of another breed of man, rustling secrets, fabled antiquity, the New Jerusalem revealed for a flickering frightened moment. I have read her testimony, memories of other times and of that land, Atlantis, lost and living now only so long as Mary Jane Dana lives.

She spoke of her patient: "She's drowning in phlegm, Mother, the poor old thing. She was conscious this morning for a few moments and asked for Ovaltine."

"Ah," Mrs. Dana said.

"At nine o'clock I couldn't find her pulse at all. That's how thready it was, Mother, you would not believe it. And you know I'm no slouch when it comes to pulses."

"Oh, I know that, dear."

Mary Jane slumped on the sofa, knees apart; her tight slacks and jersey bulged with muscles. "I'm sure I won't be on tonight. I'm afraid this case is terminated, Mother."

"You need the rest, dear."

"Do you play bridge?" Mary Jane asked, turning now on me her quite ordinary eyes. I said I did. "Good. I've got to take a little nap now but let's play bridge this evening. It is such a pleasure when a fourth turns up. And you'll like Leroy Flickinger. We play three-handed with him, Mother and I, when there's no fourth, which is most of the time." She stretched and yawned. "You'll find Leroy very interesting. He is writing a book on missing links and he is full of lore."

"Your bed's turned down," her mother said as she made for the stairs. "I aired the sheets. Sleep well, dear. I'll phone Leroy and ask him over."

From some other part of the house then I heard Mrs. Dana's voice on the telephone, talking to Leroy Flickinger, her voice full of a spurious excitement, the trembling that overcomes some women when speaking to a potential son-in-law. Palms of my hands rubbing with delicate erotic intent the rosy plush arms of my chair, I inclined toward sleep, so exhausted was I by distances, memory of maps, Mary, badlands, the plains, dying towns of the cartilage areas. Have we really come to stay? I wondered. America the complicated, the labyrinthine, tricky as the innards of an artichoke.

Yes, but are we here to stay? I mean are we really here to stay or have we only come—all of us—just for a spell, to make our fortunes and then return to the old country? Aren't we—don't you sometimes ask yourself this?—are we not going to give it back to the Indians after all? Is this for keeps? Looking at Pittsburgh, remembering the lost towns of Pennsylvania, Long Island and Ohio: the wasting villages of New England: the deadlands I drove through from Bison to Wunter, the mass-produced main streets, neon rising in a hundred thousand tubes—indication of poor health, fluctuating temperature of tuberculars, the thready pulse of dying towns. Oh we've given this continent such a terrible beating; broken it, really; kicked it where it hurts, hit it where it lives, like pirates sacking a port and leaving behind nothing but smoking ruins. Only people who did not intend to stay would have treated the land in such a way. We've plundered it, like tourists, like sailors on liberty, soldiers on leave, like people with a round-trip ticket in their pockets. Have we, I ask myself, have we, this generation of us, have we been abandoned here in the New World by careless, wicked forebears who have made their pile and their getaway and just don't give a damn for us? Blooded men they were, spoiled sons, sent off to the colonies because they got a tweeny maid in trouble; then made it big in wheat or sheep or steel and left their brood (us) behind to make our way or perish in this hard, despoliated land; while they, booted, riding crop thrusting at the tops of flowers (thwack! thwack!), promenade in cultivated parks among copies of Roman statues, sculptured hedges.

They've gone and left us, I tell you, and here we wander in our circles wondering what it's all about, restless, worried, full of unnamable anxieties: we know that something's wrong but can't quite put our finger on it. Isn't that it? Isn't it? Aren't we all waiting and yearning for someone to lead us out of the wilderness? Aren't we—let's face up to this once and for all!—frightened in this enormous country? He'd better come soon, our Moses, for I, speaking for myself now, I can't wait forever, naked in these flatlands without a stick of shade, bugged in cities, hung up in small towns, lost in the untended forests: those woodlands of ours that go on and on, unplanned and unaccounted for, jostling, elbowing trees in their thousands, growing any old which way. Sometimes I think we shall have to beat our way out blindly like Cabeza de Vaca, and trust to luck to make it to one coast or the other and take ship for a country where the people care and are not so profligate—Portugal, say, or Japan. In countries like those I have the feeling they'll make it last another thousand years or so; they cherish every clod and pebble, knowing it has got to last, that it's precious beyond price, that it's all we've got.

I'm afraid we've got the upstart's extravagance, the bad manners of the *arriviste:* something sharp-toothed and wild inside us, trying to eat its way out. Let these animals once break free and, you'll see, friend, we'll turn them loose on the whole damned world.

Again I drifted, my head falling back on the unspeakable rose plush, Mrs. Dana's special telephone voice like taffy in my ears and head. I could feel the terrible pulled sweetness of it coiling round my brain, clogging the precious cells, gray matter worth its weight in earth. I wondered whether Intelligence was on my trail, told myself to get up and look out the window, but could not move. Plush has microscopic tentacles; that is why so many never leave small towns but stick it out for a lifetime: those chairs, tempting them from store windows, finally bought, hold them prisoner like those clinging underwater plants, until they drown. Well, death by water is said to be an easy death; I gave myself to it.

Mrs. Dana woke me gently. "Why don't you let me fix you a bed," she said; and I got up, drugged with distance, and followed her up the stairs, my head just missing the knobbed wood thingumajig, relic of Victoria (My God what a distant age! Most antique of all!) that decorated the top of the doorway.

Forgetting her, I began to undress while she was still there, turning down the bed; the room had the coldness of guest rooms, of a place not much used; never mind that the general had slept here only a night ago: he gives out no warmth but consumes it all, and melts the faster for it. Fire to feed the waxworks on, *tu sais*. I fell asleep at once, cocoa-colored blanket touching my chin, and dreamed that a fragile filament surrounded and separated me from the world, a transparent cocoon. Spun for me by whom?

And at dusk she woke me, brightly, distant, from the door of the room: "Mr. Brown! Mr. Brown! Dinner is ready and Leroy is here."

When I entered the living room she was there, simpering over Leroy, a thin middle-aged man in a Henry Higgins sweater and steel-rimmed glasses. He removed the glasses as he shook hands with me, as if he wanted to keep nothing hidden. His eyes were nondescript; I looked at them, I looked at them because, after all, I had been invited to, hadn't I? But nothing was to be learned there. I turned away, embarrassed.

He asked, "Are you interested in pygmies, Mr. Brown?"

Mrs. Dana said, "I am certain Mr. Brown is interested in pygmies, Leroy, but let us eat first, please."

"They are sometimes mistaken for the Missing Link," Leroy said.

"He doesn't often get someone new to confide in," Mrs. Dana said, by way of apology.

"They are, without doubt, the oldest people on this earth of ours, but they definitely are not of the order of Missing Links," Leroy went on, ignoring her.

Mary Jane entered at this point. "Are you talking about the pygmies, dear?" she asked, not unkindly.

"Yes, I am, Mary Jane. How are you feeling?" He kissed her on the cheek. They were of identical height. This made me sad.

"How are things at the bank, dear?"

"Just fine."

"Leroy is head teller at the Wunter First National," Mrs. Dana said, leading us now toward the dining room. She pointed out my chair. "I'm a proud cook, Mr. Brown, and expect you to do justice."

"It was all this talk of 'little people' on the space ships that led me to my investigation of the pygmies, Mr. Brown. Let me tell you, sir: what I discovered was an eye-opener."

"Pass the peas, Leroy."

"What would you say, Mr. Brown, if I were to tell you that the pygmy has existed since the Miocene Era? And that he has been living on this earth 33,000,000 years? Perhaps *that* will give you some idea of his advanced age, as a people. We know that space flights have been going on for at least 3500 years. If they've been going on for that long, there's every chance they've been going on for longer."

Mary Jane agreed. "According to my dreams . . ."

"Let me say this to you, Mr. Brown—and this is a sober, considered opinion—I'm a down-to-earth-type man—I believe the pygmies were left here, originally. I believe they were originally from elsewhere and sent here to do a job of work; and then, for one reason or another, had to be left behind and never got picked up again. Who knows what supra-terrestrial cataclysm caused those ships never to return for the ancestors of today's pygmy!"

"Gravitational shifts," Mary Jane said. "We know it had to do with Venus."

"Sometimes," Leroy said, putting down his fork, "sometimes I look at a photo portrait of a pygmy—a photo, mind you—and I am moved to tears. Let me tell you why: the sadness, the *sad*ness of a pygmy's face moves me to tears. I think the pygmy is the saddest man on this our earth. He has been waiting. He has been waiting for aeons. In the jungles he waited for the ships to come and take him home. Now he knows they are not coming, and that is why the pygmy is the saddest of men."

"I think he may have given up too soon," I said.

"Then you believe They are coming?" Mary Jane said.

I said yes. (Well, I was among friends; I could feel that.)

"Oh, I'm so glad," Mrs. Dana said.

"I'd like to believe it, Mr. Brown, but I have no evidence of it."

"Yes," Mary Jane said, "Leroy has doubts." She was unhappy about this, as if she were certain it was the kind of thing that, according to women's magazines, might cause trouble later.

"I'm not leaving this table until everyone has seconds," Mrs. Dana said.

"Your original pygmy," Leroy said, "was from outer space. I am convinced of that. I believe it was this extra-terrestrial little man who worked the mines, for example, at Zimbabwe. That may surprise you, but let me put to you a few simple, straightforward questions."

"I'll just serve the coffee."

"I'll do it, Mother."

"Just you sit there, Mary Jane. Coffee is *my* work."

"No coffee for me, thank you," Leroy said. "*Now,* we know that over 300,000,000 dollars' worth of gold was taken out of the Zimbabwe mines. Where did it go? To what country was it exported? How? Thousands of men worked those mines, yet there is no burial ground, no remains have been found. Why were the dead taken away? Where were they taken? Who *were* those people? Your average archaeologist has not got a clue. Zimbabwe is almost three hundred miles from the coast; yet there are no roads and there is no evidence there ever were any. How then were those big granite blocks brought there, and how was the gold shipped out? These are only some of the questions that spring to mind, Mr.

Brown; questions, I might add, that your average archaeologist doesn't bother his head over."

"So true," Mary Jane said; but no one paid attention to her, aware that when she was not in trance she knew nothing and differed not at all from the housewife down the street. I admire her, but I wouldn't want to be in her shoes: valuable only when unconscious, a mere hostage, a mouthpiece, like a delegate to the UN. Don't you feel sorry for them?—all the trappings but never the reins of power. Poor souls. The Africans, at least, get to dress up for it; but the Westerners must try to make it in ordinary pin stripes. Well, never mind, it is a matter of no importance; there they evade those primary concerns which will (quite literally) make us or break us.

The card table was decorated with the reproduction of a fox-hunting scene: surreal, remote; like the UN Building it could as well be some futuristic scene, so past it is. Mary Jane dealt with skill; the bidding was fast; everyone played better than he had eaten. Food was available any time; but bridge, four-handed, was a rare thing and they went at it like gluttons. Leroy nevertheless continued with his lecture; and it was nonetheless passionate for having been memorized—not committed to memory, perhaps, but impressed upon memory by so many recitings of it, mostly to himself, in his room, alone, at night: looking out over the great hall, the hushed sea ho ho of faces: Ladies and gentlemen, I am here tonight . . . (Our imagined audiences, accumulating over the years, must now number in the millions, eh?)

"Let me say this to you, Brown: the pygmies, clearly, were the earliest colonists of this earth. They were brought here with the tools for mining and the technical know-how to erect those buildings at Zimbabwe and sink the shafts. Obviously the gold was needed on the home planet for some purpose or other, probably something that had nothing to do with money. It is inconceivable that in a society so advanced, money, as such, would any longer be useful."

"Three clubs," Mrs. Dana said.

"Double. No, it was definitely needed for some scientific purpose. Now here is what I'd like to try: just as, under hypnosis, Mary Jane here reveals memories of Atlantis, so too, under the same conditions, I believe a pygmy would have a lot to tell us. But here's the problem:

who but pygmies can speak the pygmy tongue? It's a sealed language, Brown. Do you know whether it would be possible to go out and live among them for a year or two and learn their language? Or is there, do you know, a Christian pygmy somewhere who has learned to speak English? That's the problem, Brown. Table, table, Mary Jane!"

"Sorry."

"I wrote my congressman. Well, I didn't know where else to turn. And asked him did he know, or did he know *where* I can find *out* about a Christian pygmy who speaks English. He wrote and told me—oh, he was as helpful as he could be, I suppose—that he had put my question to the Smithsonian and they had replied in the negative. They knew of no Christian pygmies. Down one, doubled, Mother Dana; too bad. Yes, Brown, if I could get hold of a Christian pygmy, I'd be in business."

"You should try the missionaries, Leroy, as I have often told you."

Leroy shook his head. "No help, Mary Jane; they'd be no help. Can you imagine a missionary just turning over to me a Christian pygmy? Not on your life! He'd want to know what I want him for, how long I intended keeping him, et cetera. If I were your average missionary and had a Christian pygmy who spoke English I can assure you that I'd be very careful who I lent him out to. Now suppose, just for the sake of argument, that I found such a missionary, a missionary with a Christian and English-speaking pygmy, and I told him what my purposes are. Do you think he'd be sympathetic? Oh yes, maybe if I had a Ph.D. from Harvard like your average archaeologist. But lend a pygmy to Leroy Flickinger, first teller at the Wunter First National?—Not by a long shot."

"Two hearts," Mrs. Dana said.

I smiled back at her. And why not? I suspected even then that would be all I had to give her. She gave me now, just above the fan of her cards, the secret cat smile; elbows and the white of her arms guarding her girl breasts. Menacing; like being under the guns of a fortress; when she moved it was more than a mere turning: she swiveled on ball bearings like a gun mount. Boom! Boom! A man could die of such grapeshot, get a head full of it and fall at the very gate of the fort. (Where was *Mr.* Dana? What had happened to *him?*)

Later, around midnight, perhaps because I was a guest, perhaps because she felt left out, Mary Jane went into trance (slipped into it as if it were an old shoe) and described (stuttering at times; odd) the glories of Atlantis. Memories of that submerged land floated to the surface of her unconscious and broke, like bubbles, into speech. The soul, she testified, found it more easy to express itself in those days, because this first race of men was closer to God in time and still felt His shaping touch. The third eye, keen and sensitive, youthful, worked creative and psychic marvels. Atlanteans lived surrounded by monstrosities: physically and mentally deformed men, Earth's first unfortunate children, who coupled with animals. Some among the Atlanteans, fallen into bad ways, mated with monstrosities and the race began to lose its purity. Thus was caste and class brought into the world; and dissension. Grotesques, men with hooves, tails, horns—some with feathers—began to proliferate. (See the Egyptian bas-reliefs for confirmation of this.)

"What about Lemuria, dear?" Mrs. Dana asked in a normal voice.

Mary Jane replied: "Lemuria was the first to go. Great explosion; pockets of gas in eruption. Fissures appeared, the earth split and broke apart. Because man had fallen into evil this came about. Lemuria sank into the sea. Then Atlantis went. The Caribbean islands are all that remain of it. Relics of its glory lie at the bottom of the Sargasso Sea."

Leroy held her hand.

She said, "The Atlanteans were well versed in the secrets of electronics and atomic energy, which they used for peaceful purposes and for rejuvenation. A few remained true to the high ideals but the many fell into evil: sexual perversions, sloth, adultery and corruption."

"It's the same old story everywhere," Mrs. Dana said, shaking her head.

"By 30,000 B.C. it all began to come to an end. Using the sun's energy to charge crystal, they had learned to rejuvenate their bodies. But this knowledge came to be ill-used. God's wrath, God's wrath, God's wrath . . ."

"Yes, dear?"

"God's wrath that day of wrath . . ."

"She's coming out," Leroy said.

Mrs. Dana got up and smoothed her slacks. "I'd better make some sandwiches. When she comes out, she's always hungry."

Mary Jane opened her eyes and put her head on Leroy's shoulder. "Stone cities white, shining." She yawned and shook her head. "I'm so hungry, Leroy dear."

"Mother Dana is preparing melted cheese sandwiches, Mary Jane."

We talked of Atlantis while we waited for the sandwiches. Like us, Mary Jane knew of it only what she had read: transcriptions of her own testimony, in the main. "Why was I chosen?" she asked. I felt sorry for her, knowing the burden of it; overwhelmed with sadness, I took her hand. Leroy smiled. "There," he said, as if he were handing me a bundle of fivers through his little grilled window at the bank.

"How far we'd be advanced today if only we had not lost the third eye," he said wistfully.

"No use talking about what might have been," Mary Jane said. "Here we are and we've got to find our way back."

"I know that," he said, thinking (I'm sure) of his pygmy full of secrets.

"Through reincarnation Atlantis still makes its influence felt," she said, "though as a nation it ceased to exist by 9000 B.C. The spirit of Atlantis will rise again, Leroy dear, just you see if it doesn't."

Then we fell into silence and I felt the chilling wind; unnamable presentiments caused anguish in my soul. In a world of monsters how shall the pure survive? Oh they're pulling us down, they're pulling us down; we'll sink into the sea; those walls will buckle and submerge us. Fifty fathoms deep we'll lie then, a marvel to fishes, a prodigy of silt. Wavering architecture, watery dream of achievement and loss. How dim, distant and cold the sun will be. I shivered; the loss of the world struck to my bones.

Understanding, this surprising teller, at the door, after sandwiches and beer, leaving, took my hand and said: "But when ye shall see the abomination of desolation, standing where it ought not, then let them that be in Judea flee to the mountains."

"Yes, yes," I said.

"Then shall he send his angels, and shall gather together his elect from the four winds, from the uttermost parts of the earth, to the uttermost part of Heaven."

"Oh yes," I said..

And Mrs. Dana said to me, "Then you really think They are coming? I have often thought about it; but I can never see them as pygmies, can you? I see them tall, blond and blue-eyed. They'll be perfect in every way. Well, I live in hope, Mr. Brown. I'm waiting, just like everybody else. I don't for a minute think I'm one of the elect, but I know that I am the mother of one and believe I'll be accepted among Them in one capacity or another."

Of course I was helpless to answer and inwardly cried tears of desperation and assaulted my mind with this question: William, William, what can you do for these people?

twenty-two

SNUCK OUT like a thief, at daybreak, and quit that town. Left behind no trees and Leroy Flickinger, Elks, Moose, Lions; dreaming Mary Jane Dana, pale as a haemophiliac, blood-let and trepanned by an ancient past. Better to leave it buried, perhaps; after all, what do we really know of Atlantis? Caution is sometimes to be recommended. And the Missus? She who leans on her elbows and whited arms, has claws for hands, asks riddles, carried M.J. (puissant babe) in her tight flat little womb? Up by nine, surely, for flapjacks ho ho and the day's first soap opera. In Wunter, what else? In Wunter her life must be full of Musak. She walks in it.

I felt fine (should you wonder), rested and buoyant, ready for anything. How I amaze myself; the more so because, young, I relished my youth and the very smell of myself and saw a man of forty as a man done and finished with. Now I am there at that incredible age, and find it full of juice and vigor. What rich veins yet remain to be tapped in me? I'd turn on (not a bit scared) every spigot in the book if I could only find them; and at seventy-two (why doubt it?) still be thumping with the best and, perhaps, develop a sweet tooth for little girls. Become a pincher. Become (O what delight!) a Dirty Old Man.

At seventy-five or thereabouts I'll practise a loose-kneed walk, the slightly uncoordinated movement of a man who's raised a bit of hell in his day (and had to pay for it); wet-lipped, hair dyed a patently false black, two perfectly round spots of rouge on my cheeks, cunning dentures clamped to my gums, and with a nicely scented (it's mint, I think) breath. I will probably expose myself in parks and playgrounds and lure them to my room with Baby Ruth bars.

Not so far-fetched, is it? I am a man—as the police reports would put it—a man *of no fixed address.* We end up that way: in that mungy room, or knighted by the queen. It is the letch for power takes us that route; we travel, all of us, Lord Rutherford and the Dirty Old Men, the same road; but we see different signs or see the same ones but read them differently. It's all a matter of response: my two plus two is your two plus two. But what's four to me and what's four to you? Ah ha. Sometimes (often, really) I see four as a startled openmouthed bird and can count the beats of its frightened heart right through the feathers. Laugh if you like, friend.

At noon I came to the town of Ferris where I spoke to a barber named Laverne Weed, one of Oliver's parishioners, a man with a two-chair shop and no assistant. "Barbers are a dying race," he said, but did not seem worried about it—one of those, you would think at first glance, for whom the world dies when he dies; no sense of indebtedness to the future. But then, in answer to my question, he said, "Why yes, the general was here and left a message for you"—and he led me into the small bare-board room behind his shop where he worked on the model of a fantastic (and unworkable) Jacob's ladder, a structure of his own design, cunning but without wit. The model was made of matchsticks dipped in gold radiator paint; set on a table it aspired to the ceiling in a stiff-necked way, and slightly askew, like an aging prima donna straining in the strong wind of an Italian.

He looked for the general's message amid a clutter of

old letters, circulars, and magazines: a heaving mass of papers that lapped out of open drawers and leaked from the pigeonholes of a roll-top desk. While he searched—stopping to leaf through a 1929 copy of *Cap'n Billy's Whiz Bang*—he spoke of this golden structure. Pointing to its splayed legs he said, "I'll sink 'em a mile deep in concrete and bury 'em in mud. That way it'll rock as the world rocks; the mud will serve as shock absorbers and keep it from breaking. I've written to all the best engineers in Omaha and Bison, city people but they know what they're talking about. They all say the same thing: it is feasible. I'll show you their letters."

Oh, the yearning for heaven! It strikes in strange places, does it not? Chiliasts, Cathars, Waldensians; Rilke aghast at the sight of Toledo; and this barber in Ferris with his little round belly, clown's flat feet, nose like something crying out to be buried (Don't worry, it will flower!), dressed in a dentist's white tunic, a butcher's boater covering his baldness.

Cigar like a wand or a pencil, he drew a circle in the air. "It'll work," he said, "oh yes, it'll work all right. And think what it'll do for the state, Brown. Biggest thing since Mt. Rushmore. It's the unions I'm up against. We could hire Iroquois Indians—all we wanted—for the high work, but can you see the unions giving a go-ahead? Not on your life. And the Iroquois is one hard-working Indian, let me tell you. Give him a cigar and he's a happy Indian. I spoke to the marshal; he's a federal man. Said he'd give me all the help he could. So here I am, Brown, with all the power of Washington behind me and the unions arrayed against me. Solid wall. I'm fighting them tooth and nail. If I had a million dollars I'd start digging tomorrow and tell George Meany to fish or cut bait."

He left the desk and led me by the elbow to the wall where the map of his state was tacked and stretched tight as a skin set to cure; a fur of dust, stirred by his breath, curled and shifted. In the state's four corners were four red *x*'s. "Right here's where we sink the foundations." He tapped each *x* with his little finger and smiled at them fondly, as if they were his issue. "Fortunately for us, this state forms a perfect square—almost; except for that iddy biddy corner down there. But we won't worry about that, Brown. We can square off the foundations! No trouble about that. Hello there, Duane."

A tall man, sunken-cheeked, wearing ornately embroidered cowboy boots, had entered and now leaned in the doorway like a forgotten brace. Laverne introduced him to me.

"Duane Hardtog, county surveyor."

"What've you got for lunch?" the surveyor asked, his hollow cheeks puffing like bladders as he spoke, as if speech were so much gas.

Laverne ignored him. "Four soaring arches spanning the state," he said, gazing at the glittering model, that golden swan hunched over the deal table. "Topped by a golden latticework of jointed metal. Build it up in easy stages. Hydraulic elevators. Restaurants and rest houses at every five-hundredth level, designed in the manner of a Swiss chalet. I've got plans."

I edged back toward the desk, hoping this would remind him that I was waiting.

"Reminds me of the Eiffel Tower," Duane said. "Bigger, of course."

"How you been feeling, Duane, these days?" Laverne asked. "Made any bets lately?" His smile revealed malice and a gold tooth.

"Be like living under the Third Avenue El," Duane said. "The whole state. I just don't see it, Laverne."

Laverne smiled, full of tolerance, unmoved by the disbelief of others. "Oh ye of little faith, Duane."

"What've you got for lunch?" the surveyor asked again.

"Twenty years," Laverne said to me. "Given the money we could be up there in twenty years. And if they want to shoot their rockets off the top—well, I'll let them. Figure it out yourself, Brown—at a dollar a head? Why, you'd have 'em lined up from here to the Kansas border. And in the summer months, farther than that." He was silent for a moment, lost in his vision, the cigar dead in his hand—Duane asked him what he was having for lunch—then he said, "We'd have to control the atmosphere in the elevators. I'm going to write to the Otis people about that very thing. Otherwise you'd have a lot of tourists complaining."

"Sure would," Duane said.

"When did the general leave?" I asked.

"Bends, and things like that. I wrote a letter to Walter Reuther and told him what I thought of him."

"Never answered you, didn't he?" Duane said.

"You got vested interests everywhere, Brown."

"Do you think you could find the general's letter now?"

"What's for lunch, Laverne?"

The barber took his lunch pail from the shelf; when he walked, the golden model shivered, fearing the worst. He pushed aside a log jam of several hundred gilded matches, put down the black tin box and opened it. Duane gave up his job as brace and entered the room; the wall stood.

"Good old Myrt," Duane said.

I knew at once I was in the presence of ritual.

Laverne took out a thermos, then a sandwich wrapped in aluminum foil.

"She's a good little packer," Duane said.

"Yes, she is." Carefully, he unwrapped the sandwich and, more than ever like a dentist now, opened it slowly at one corner, leaned toward it and narrowed his eyes; cautious, lest it snap shut on his fingers. Then he closed it, sat back and smiled.

Duane advanced another step. "What kind of sandwich she make you today, Laverne?"

"Philadelphia cream cheese," Laverne said in a non-committal voice. "With sliced olives." There was something like triumph in the latter.

Duane shook his head. "Good old Myrt. With olives?"

"With sliced olives."

Duane left.

Laverne rewrapped the sandwich. "It's the only way to get rid of him," he said. He put the sandwich back in the box. "Thought it was going to be salami today. Or Lebanon bologna. Haven't had salami this week yet. Duane thought it was going to be salami too; I could tell by his face. He came in here yesterday and butter wouldn't melt in his mouth; said, 'Bet it's going to be salami.' " Laverne laughed aloud at the memory of it; his body shook, gold tooth flashed. " 'I'll take that bet,' says I. He won't bet with me now for a while yet, Duane won't."

He looked up at his work. "It's all in the foundations, Brown. You give yourself a big enough foundation and you can go as high as it suits you." He opened the lunch pail again and offered me half his sandwich; but I said I had to be leaving. He nodded. It was becoming obvious that he was in no hurry to have me leave; I was a new audience. He tilted his chair and looked up at the top of the tower. "I'll go halfway, Brown; I'll meet Them halfway. I'd go the whole way, only this state isn't big enough. Last year I thought of going to California; I toyed with the state of California for a while there. But it's too narrow. California is too narrow, Brown. Pennsylvania is perfect in size and shape but it's honeycombed with old coal mines. Danger of cave-ins. I was in Wilkes-Barre once; also spent a weekend in Forty Fort, a nearby suburb of Wilkes-Barre." He shook his head. "Like walking on eggshells, Brown."

"Yes. About that . . ."

"No, says I to myself, I'll stay right here, I'll stay right where I am. People know me here. I am known and I'd be missed. You sure you don't want half this sandwich?"

"I've got to be moving on," I said. "About that message from the general . . ."

He gave me up—he had said all he had to say, apparently—and he made a last assault on the desk, waded right in and plucked the general's message (he had known all along where it was) from between the pages of an old copy of *Liberty* magazine; an article on technocracy was advertised on the cover. "Well, what do you know," he said, handing me the letter. Still holding *Liberty,* he began to read Princess Kropotkin's woman's page, chuckling over a recipe.

The general's message read as follows:

> TO: The Man Who Is Following Me.
>
> SUBJECT: A Warning.
>
> Who are you? What do you want? If you are what I think you are, I'll have you whipped. Be warned. At 0800 hours, this date, I saw your face in my rear-view mirror. I will know you if I see you again. I am not without power.

I put this letter in my pocket, only later realizing I should have left it for the man it was intended to reach—that well-combed, blond, blue-eyed young gentleman from Intelligence—and said goodby to Laverne Weed.

Left him to his (our) curious American dream: salvation with a high margin of profit—suckers lined up to the Kansas border—heaven at cost plus six per cent; a St. John of the Cross with itching palms. The delicious science, yes, but gone bad in the badlands, at the continent's very heart, there where boredom is the disease incurable and even the soul's legitimate longings become bastardized. I drove down the machine-made main street, which was also the state highway (no privacy anywhere!), and away from Ferris.

Oh the unnecessary small towns of our great land! Like Venus, they drain our energy.

twenty-three

YES, I CLOSED the door of my Plymouth and hoisted sail; launched myself, drove without stopping all day and, that night, for a couple hours, slept on the back seat and cast off again before dawn; hours later saw the sun coming up on my left. Due south. Part pilgrim, part Columbus, I wanted to find brotherhood and gold too. Hands lashed to the wheel I drove through towns where contacts waited, names on Oliver's list, underworld guides I did not really need. We have maps, don't we? I kept myself awake by whistling and stopped for coffee every hundred miles or so; that way I was able to pass through Beagle and Dortsville without seeing, in the one, Mrs. Alice Hunter and, in the other, Oscar Zeitz. Will never be their distinguished guest from back East; will never know their particular longing. If there's a pygmy-man in Wunter, what might one not find in Beagle? Farewell, Alice Hunter, go find yourself another. I was, you see, courting exhaustion by driving and driving myself so; it is only through exhaustion that the true renewal comes: that second wind of intoxicating sweetness.

Crossing a corner of Louisiana I found it: an hour after stopping at a diner for coffee I found it and turned around, drove back to that diner and looked for the man I was certain had been with me. Why had I left him behind? Oh how bad of me, how forgetful! But who was he? I did not know, yet was certain a friend had been with me and I had left him behind. I went back for him. Looked for him at the diner, ordered another coffee, and drove on; he wasn't there. Later I had the feeling it was Oliver who had been with me and could even smell the odor of his pipe and tweeds and sanctity. Then I thought *No!*—and I drove off the road and stopped to think about this—no, it was Nancy, the ex-nurse, the general's widow-wife. Former troubler of my Government Issue dreams. Had she been with me? I drove back, slowly, along the highway and looked for her, had the feeling she was walking now, trying to catch up with me, that she stumbled in panic on the soft shoulder, blue chips in her bindle, poor widow and orphan. I'll find you, Nancy dear, I cried; and gunned the dirty engine. And then as suddenly gave it up and pulled over, slept for an hour in that corner of Louisiana, and with my head on the steering wheel, cushioned by my crossed arms, in an attitude of prayer, dreamed of Thomas Jefferson: saw his powdered face and the grosgrain ribbons on his knees. He knew; he had believed that west of the Missouri were great salt flats and monsters of prehistory. "William," he said, and touched my shoulder with his stiff fingers, "you must go seek it out and save us all." His touch was kingly, flat as a sword; and when I woke I felt like one of those young knights just released from the all-night vigil in the royal chapel. How powerful then was my right arm as I turned the key and started out again!

fifth proclamation

¶ We're in a lonely spot, folks. In our part of the stellar universe the nearest star is 25 million million miles away.

twenty-four

IN WHERE was it?—in Oklahoma, I think; in Wherewasit, Oklahoma, I think it was, sky and landscape suddenly clamped shut around me, turned inscrutable; a sinister mythic dust storm, falling out of the thirties. In fact,

I saw it coming but it was no bigger than the size of your hand and I thought nothing of it, figured it to lie on the horizon and wait for me, that then I'd pass it by and think no more of it. I should have known. Flashing, it struck and left my sails in tatters. Frightful; I gripped the wheel tight and held to the course as well as I was able. Those clouds—that one great cloud, rather—was engraved in steel; flattened to the page it would serve to illustrate Dante or any other account of space travel.

In the midst of this, caught the eye in my rear-view mirror of someone in the back seat: dark man, balding. (Realized only later he had a boy with him; family resemblance.) Stopped at a gas station; went to the men's room; they were gone when I came back. I think I did that man and the boy some great service; have the feeling I rescued them from sure disaster. Swart; gypsies perhaps, or circus people. No matter; I was pleased to be of service.

The picketing Quakers; I thought of them and all I'd left behind: the laboratory, Greely and Doris, my flat and Mary Kovarchuk's presence there. I could have lived out my life there in that not unpleasant round: Stella once a week, the comforts of the familiar. Bugged by Walz and the people from Intelligence, I could have quit the lab and made my way. Other colleagues had; they left to take better-paying jobs, and easier ones, as advisers to builders of fallout shelters, or they hit the lecture circuit for the atomic energy people or went to one of those institutes, riverine, tax-free. Like some of them I might have ended up a TV personality, mouth full of encouraging words, jolly in the face of death by the millions.

Why didn't I go that way instead of this, this way so unfashionable and in company with people not my sort? I could have learned the vocabulary, could have got it down as pat as Max and Herman: *megadeath, counterforce as insurance, credible first-strike capability, bonus damage, calculated win, postattack blackmail, automatic overkill, doomsday machine.* You see how easy it is? It could be packaged; a child of twelve could learn it; it has, in fact, been packaged and grown men sell it. Biggest thing since Parcheesi. These men have committed the greatest betrayal of all: they've sold reality down the river. And us. This land. And the world, that sweet apple full of juice and seed, pith, meat. Tap it with your fingernail and hear that reassuring *thuck,* so promising and lovely. Herman, Max, Chet and Walter, now hear this: We are each of us responsible for the use to which we put our lives. No, don't turn away, man—I've got you by the lapel—don't turn away—you, salesman of disaster and the safety that can never be manufactured, step up here, join me, make your decision now, become (like me) the apple's witness, agent, defender, protector.

A final word, gentlemen:

Gentlemen, we must become gods and guide, cherish, fondle in our hands and warm like brandy this sweet-apple world we have made by our recognition and given meaning to.

twenty-five

VOYAGING LIKE this I should have kept a log and stopped once a day, gone up to the tilting bridge to shoot the sun and set down long. and lat., and shorthand reminders of images and encounters; simple matter then to work up the notes. A quick neat job it would have been if only I'd had the forethought. Now here I have to give my all to memory and pay it the tithe of sweat, and to no avail: I confess it, friend: I cannot remember one day or town from another and must employ a logic that has little to do with chronology or the map's exactitude. That map, marked, towns circled in red, lies spread before me, held flat by the bow of my predecessor's violin (Greely, dear soul, forgive!). Here are towns: Beasly, Thonsville, New Warsaw, Waxton, Duco, Harvey, East Bend, Hare.

Was it in Beasly then that leaving the diner the fat man hailed me from his leatherette booth, crying "Brown! Brown!" Obsessed by destination I had given up Oliver's list, but the word had gone out (somehow; was it Oliver who told them? the barber in Ferris? the bank teller and pygmy fancier of Wunter? who?) and now they waited for me, hungry for companionship in those accidental towns where everyone knows everyone and nothing is important unless it is local. "I thought it must be you," he said when I turned, and he rose from his hamburger special to come and take me by the shoulder, as if he feared I might run away and leave him alone again. The thought of it crumpled his face. Sad as a pygmy he was, this lost soul name of Joseph Light here in his Zimbabwe of Beasly.

Speech burst from him; sluice gate opened, it poured out with enough force to run all the washing machines in the county. Accounted for his fat, too; he stored up words in his belly; unused words gave him girth, they hibernated in him from one year to the next. Strangers, not seasons, woke them. They smashed against each other, cracked, broke, overlapped. Caught in that torrent I waited in the shelter of my fatigue and my detachment. I was like that diner's counterman who polished now the coffee urn that needed no polishing: I was engaged in the unnecessary, a pursuit that causes reality to slip away (it is an angular, jolting, unsmooth movement, as if it were screwed to a ratchet and removed from us one tooth at a time, thack, thack, thack.)

Poor man, he made me feel like Mr. Right. "I've been waiting for you, William Brown," he said. "I've been waiting for you. I knew that sooner or later someone like you would come here, stop, and talk to me. The general was here yesterday. He is nothing but a leader. Only in a backward—not to say primitive—society like ours is there a place for him. It is you, Brown—may I call you William?—you we need."

All this in the odor of frying fats; and walls of posters: the cola people pushing grilled cheese sandwiches and franks-and-beans; and the silent jukebox, its colors churning, as if silence causes an anguish in its innards; it demands buffered dimes for comfort and release from pain, stomach distress, hyperacidity and all the ills that man's been made heir to (the pills come first, then the malaise; packaging takes primacy over mankind).

He had a fat man's unnatural elgance of movement and used his hands in limpid gestures; like slow-motion birds; as if the air were water.

He said, "I have ideas that will disturb the sleep of the world, for which I am responsible. Just to be born, William, to come into the world is to be brought up on charges. I am, like you, William, engaged in the great *new* debate. The old one ended when the world was made. Imagine how long and how hard-fought that debate must have been: to make or not to make this world of men. I feel its reverberations still, William: the charge and sabre-clash of titanic ideas.

"Now we must create it anew. That is our task, that handful of us, men like you and me. The world must be made to be the location of our recovery.

"I know the kind of man you are, William Brown. You are Prince Henry, the Great Navigator. Do you know that his tutor once said to him: 'You want to attempt things beyond the power of men.' The truth of man, that is our goal, what we must achieve, our highest task.

"Ah, William, if only I knew how to set about it, if only I knew. Ideas keep me awake, the longing for perfection. You have that selfsame itch, lad, yes; I recognized you by it; it is our sign.

"Blueprints of great machines appear in my dreams. Is it not interesting that the information systems of the digital computers are so amazingly like the genetic code of the chromosomes?

"I have the spastic's yearning to get rid of my body. By a process of eidetic reduction I have shrugged off the transcendental Ego. Now I ask you, William, where does that leave me? I know that I am at the very heart of the matrix of something or other, something immense and infinite as freedom.

"All I need is order, a way of coding my insights and ideas; then to build that great machine and feed it with the issue of my mind, the flux of experience, the effluvium of my dreams. I see it with a handle that has only to be cranked. Then a great tongue of answers, all we have been seeking, will pour forth. A new fragrance will then surround the world, bringing salvation.

"The times are ripe for us, lad; the skies are full of signs; so much thought must have an issue. Think of the power banked behind the likes of us; us, the underground thinkers who have for centuries been wearing away the rock of vested things.

"We are the power-to-be, William; we are, we are. Don't you feel that in your blood and in your bones? I do. I feel it. And it cannot be borne for too long, kept bottled up. The time must soon come, very soon it must, or we will be hustled into desperate acts and suffer yet another setback. I can still hear the cries and smell the burnt flesh of those they called *witches*. And the excommunicated hunted alchemists, and those who learned to fly. Like Simon Magus who was brought to naught by Peter's prayers. They were thought to be of the Devil's party, you know; this in spite of the fact that the Psalmist prayed to be granted wings like a dove. And later the Inquisitors found that Galileo's theories had no place in the Christian creed, *no place,* William! Think of it!

"It's all backing up on them, lad. What's coming will make the Reformation look like a tea party, or like salvation itself. The era of aberrant religions is approaching, has already arrived, in fact. No more 'groaning in travail,' eh, lad? We know now what we're praying *for,* don't we? Yes, we have entered the Era of the Increase of Monsters, as the Indian legend puts it. The time for the holy No has arrived; we have given up waiting, merely *waiting* for salvation; now all others must, too, and join us in seeking it, become activists, God's hunters and stalkers and beaters."

"I must go now," I said.

He nodded sadly and asked if I would stop to see him on my way back. I told him I did not know if I would be coming back. "I may not be coming back," I said. His eyes opened with discovery; his enormous body had thrilled to the meaning of my words. "Take me!" he said, grasping the sleeve of my shirt. "Take me with you!"

"You know I cannot," I said, speaking with as much gentleness and kindness as I was able to summon up; and at the same time turning, moving away from his importuning hand.

He folded his hands on the table, a beaten schoolboy. "Then try to send me a message, lad," he pleaded.

"I'll try."

He smiled his gratitude and looked at me with lover's eyes, silently offering blind service, endless devotion, all and everything. "William Brown, you are pursuing the vocation of danger." He offered this like a valedictory, his voice gone rich and juicy; and he closed his eyes to indicate joy inexpressible. "The most fruitful and enjoyable way of living one's life is to live dangerously."

And ambiguously, I added silently; but smiled modestly—that is to say, not modestly at all.

He said, saying it almost to my back as I left that place, in my haste to be gone, to reach Twelvepalms (not rudeness, I swear, but obsession whelmed me), "William Brown, you are more to be envied than any man on this earth."

Of course I did not need *him* to tell me that.

And I went out to my car. Thought about the highway, that concrete spill disgorged from some horrendous snaggled mouth on the East Coast, ignoring all obstacles until only the Pacific brings shame and brings it to a stop. Binds us together? Nonsense! Attenuates us, rather; draws us out beyond our strength, rather; unnatural as a dachshund, that is what we are: need a million little wheels to keep our belly from sagging and the vertebrae straight. Nasty business, bigness.

And I went out to my car. Pebbles crunched underfoot like a mighty breakfast food. Thought of all the two-toned cars on the highway. Must face it, I told myself; must enter that stream. Had I (have you) ever left it? We are born in it, live lives bumper to bumper, and die that way, backed up in a fluid stasis from ocean to ocean. It is a cushioned, shock-absorbing illusion—not the cars, it's the road that moves; we are made fast to it. It's a giant amusement park for children, this Disneyland of ours; even the shelters have tellys and wall-to-wall carpeting. Designed for living, *tu sais*. I heard the hiss and roar of the cars as the road flew by, saw their rolling frightened eyes, manes whipping in the wind. Awful. How could I reenter now that I was safely out? We make such a mighty wind, don't we? Pause and listen: the hot tires, their sound of frying, as if they are being cooked on Earth's skillet; the protest and whine of motors; horn's sudden startled alarm. Looking at us, what must others see? An orderly stampede. Other nations step out of the way, point toward the precipice history always prepares. They know. They point: *That way! that way!* Certain we'll go. You'll see, friend, yes I'm afraid you will, yes there is an abyss big enough for us, a Grand Canyon filled to the brim with time immemorial that splendid solution.

That was the night before my arrival in Twelvepalms. It was in this way that I made the crossing of the continent (or nearly) and found myself there at last; found also I was one of many who had been called. The general, young Heffernan, Greely, Sr., and a hundred more, not including the men from Intelligence. Twelvepalms—all of it, the hotel, the grotto of meditation, the landing field (unused, thus far), the motel cabins—was owned by Harold Brice. I had never seen him before but spotted him at once, his vulpine smile the giveaway. He had the professional handshake of his kind. "Just in time, Mr. Brown," he said.

In the grotto the convocation was beginning. Willie Lee Flowers, rector of the Second Church of Christ, Astronaut, stood in the pulpit of rock that water and time had cut for him.

I took a seat as far away from Harold Brice as I could find. I am certain I need not tell you it was *Melville* who said that in new countries, when the wolves are killed off, the foxes increase.

twenty-six

WE SAT on the stepped floor, like medical students in an operating theatre, on a green rug that might have been fungus feasting on the rock; over us the roof arched, rough, shining here and there where a chisel had been used to aid time in its mining. The steps made a gradual descent to the altar where Reverend Flowers, in black, his back to the facing wall, completed the simile by making his theological incision, turned back the flap, clamped it, and revealed the dessicated eschatology of his ridiculous church. Oh yes, I have no doubt we're the saving remnant, but not because of Oliver or this man Flowers or any other. When the New Jerusalem is let down from heaven it will not be in response to *their* command.

Flowers (let us say this for him) admitted as much: "Let me tell you this, friends: among the Egyptian *magi,* no priest was a true priest unless he could levitate and fly! I do not claim to have that power, folks."

He lacked power; but I shall have to grant him this: he had passion; or, perhaps, more exactly, a passionate plaintiveness. "Are we our own men?" he asked now and searched the grotto, as if looking for the answer on every face. "Who can claim himself for himself in this land of ours where the noise of money deafens? This trumpery trumpet that will wake no one from the dead but only blasts and sullies the minds of us all. They have drummed elevating thoughts out of our lives like loose women or Reds out of town. We've been mulcted, friends, mulcted and trepanned by three decades of radio and TV. We have come a long road since the day of the player piano in the parlor—the stereopticon on the round-topped lace-covered table under the Tiffany glass shade with its purple grapes and green leaves—the St. James Version in big fat readable type right there alongside it, the inside cover dutifully filled with birth and death dates. A man then knew who he was and knew who his grandfather had been. It is John Worrell Keely of Philadelphia . . ."

Applause broke out, clattered against the stone walls. Flowers, imperious, raised his hand for silence, but it went on; and even after it stopped the domed ceiling gave the echo of it back for a few seconds more. Whisper of an underground river suddenly heard in the silence then.

"It's Keely I'm thinking about, who grew up in those times and made his own dreams and rediscovered the lost power and gave it the name of Dynaspheric Force."

Keely's name always comes up. If the Church of Christ, Astronaut had a company of saints, he would be the first among them.

"What did he look like? We are told that he was a tall man. Not surprising. Have you ever noticed how the very tall die young? Basketball players and other tall men. Weak heart? Heart strain? No! It is because they aspire toward Home! They grow toward it like a flower to sunlight!

"What else do we know about John Worrell Keely? We know that in those days when men still thought for themselves and knew who they were, Keely's discovery aroused great interest. The Barnato Brothers, diamond kings of South Africa, sent a representative to see a demonstration of the man's work. They knew that what Keely had was more valuable than diamonds. (Trust the money men, eh, friends?)

"What did he have? What had Keely recovered? Nothing less than this: that the tiniest elements of matter—the molecules and atoms, the very corpuscles of matter—could be divided by *vibration!* This he rediscovered while investigating the magnetic forces that flow between earth's poles.

"A man named Seaver was the Barnato representative, come all the way from far-off South Africa to Keely's laboratory. What did he see there? He tells us: a twenty-five-horsepower motor was made to run when Keely played a note on his violin. To stop it, he played a discord.

"But when Seaver himself tried it was to no avail! Only with Keely's hand on his shoulder could the note struck by him on the violin move the motor to power. A personal force, clearly. Keely's personal vibration was needed. An ordinary violin would do, but an extraordinary hand on the bow was required.

"Why? Because this secret was never intended for the many! Because this secret was never intended for commercial purposes!

"Children, we have been placed on this earth to make it beautiful. Children, our salvation cannot be achieved until we have made it perfect. We are imperfect yet—I do not need to tell you—and this Etheric Force in the hands of imperfect men will avail us not but only bring the cataclysm upon us, the black wave that has in all ages threatened this wobbly little world. Friends, we will be undone before we are finished and that is the greatest sin of all, the one for which God cannot find, is not permitted to find, forgiveness.

"They've got it now! They've got the gross and earthly substitute for the sidereal force! The fifth and sixth planes of Astral Force are now in their still corrupt hands!

"Universal destruction is in hand. Friends, it is push-button close. The great continents can be riven in seconds and the ocean-seas made turbulent. The Age of Monsters approaches, sullen-mouthed beings with heaving flanks and brains the size of a pea.

"It is late! We must enlist Their intercession now or, failing that—They may have already given us up for lost and damned, and who of us could blame Them for that?—failing that, we must flee this planet They have abandoned. We must go home. We must go home and there preserve the work of a million days and hands.

"Let us pray."

sixth proclamation

¶ The world's true beginnings are unknown. The divine, celestial explosion which set matter dancing where none was before was not the beginning of all, but an event which grew out of eventless time. ¶ This possibility must therefore be faced: that the world was made behind God's back and without His permission by sly and vengeful hands.

twenty-seven

UNDER THAT VAST black and starry sky I was assailed by the total loneliness known only by one abandoned and left behind by his people. I touched my forehead, feeling for the blue tattooing of my tribe: some simple geometric design. Had I come to this desert place only to be victimized, picked over by birds of prey?

"Headache?" Brice asked from under his long-peaked cap, the kind fighting admirals wore while pacing the bridge in that antique war of which I was a veteran. Brice, owner of Twelvepalms, the fox. When such a man asks if you have a headache, you have the right to wonder if he's selling aspirins.

"A little tired perhaps," I said; but he was not interested. (He had, after all, no aspirins.)

"Can't tell you how glad I am to see you got here, Dr. Brown," he said. "I didn't want a repetition of last year. It was a circus, I can tell you. All the cuckoos turned up. You know who I mean—the ones who write books about their trips to Venus, et cetera. Even had a couple who wore capes. One man came with a Plexiglas globe on his head. People like you and the general will give us a lot of tone this year."

Brice had attached himself to me as we all filed out of the Grotto of Meditation; now, in straggling groups, clusters of three and seven, we moved toward the main building, which in this light seemed to be made of cardboard or old biscuits. "For refreshments," Brice said.

"Then it was you who phoned and told me to come to Twelvepalms," I said, said it aloud at last, saw the words (accusation and sentence both) hanging on the desert's crystal air.

Brice nodded, the peak of his cap ducking like a bird's bill seeking food in the sand. "Don't hold that against me, Dr. Brown. I didn't want another circus. Why, they made fun of us last year in a Los Angeles newspaper. For the sake of us all I couldn't let that happen again."

I looked at Brice: his face lit from beneath by moonlight reflected from the white sand, his gray stubble glittered like frost, like some animal left lying out on a cold night: his nose was pinched and there was a blueness in his lips. "Don't hold it against me, Doctor Brown."

I smiled. The fool! How like this businessman, his head full of nickels and dimes, to think that phoning me was *his* idea. Brice, I could have said, *Brice,* you are an instrument, a tool, nothing more. But he would not have understood this: a fawning innkeeper, he has a hunch his guest is a distinguished man but never dreams he's Prince Charlie come to claim a throne. (Later of course he will know; and then he'll change the name of his inn and put a plaque above the bed.)

I saw a figure detach himself and, alone, head toward his cabin: the general; I had studied his face during Reverend Flowers' sermon. His flame guttered; any strong wind now would be sufficient to undo him. At the end of the sermon, with Greystone's hand under his elbow, he got down on his knees and raised the melting button of his face toward the east, in prayer. Flowers gave him special attention, made the sign of Mercury over his upturned face. The general's mouth had fallen open and I half expected to see a ticker-tape message issue from it. Joseph Light looked like that when he said, "Take me with you! Take me!"

Greely, Sr.'s spotted hand touched my arm. "How are you, Billy?" He smiled, his pleated face tightening, the papery folds garbling the message that hid in them. "I guess you're not surprised to see me here, Billy. I got the call, you see, and I come to claim my reward. They'll have to take me back with them, Billy. I've given my whole life to this cause; yes, and my wife's too for that matter."

And your son's, I thought.

"I won't take no for an answer," Senior said. "I know my rights." He clamped his jaw and a muscle moved; like a worm it struggled to reach refuge in his ear. "I look around me at those here waiting and what I say, Billy, is this: If there's room aboard for five, I should be one of them. What do you think? What do you think?"

"There is no doubt of it, Senior."

Inside the hangarlike building—a sign over the door made a claim for it: *The Lounge*— there were plastic chairs; a small bar behind which Mrs. Brice, aproned, handed out drinks of fruit juice and ginger ale; and along one wall, old penny-candy cases containing exhibits: clumps of metal with labels reading: "Found in Brazil, released from saucer; metallurgists have been unable to analyze it." Brice's sideshow; the circus which follows should have come as no surprise to him.

"There he is," Senior said, pointing to the blond willowy man leaning on the bar, the permanent smile of the convert on his face. I had noticed him; a new face. "He's the one Junior and I told you about, Billy; come looking for the general that night at our place, gave us a sign before he left. I knew there was something about him; I spotted him. Well, now he has joined us; he is one of us now. Not the first man from Intelligence nor the last to see the error of his ways. Former enemies make good friends, Billy, as I have always said. Because they are careful with each other."

"And his partner?" I asked. (They always come in pairs.)

"Oh, Johnson's still around. Trying to get Jason to return to the fold."

I saw Greystone and moved through the clusters to his side. He was standing with Reverend Flowers and some other men, including one who was dressed in black and named Bancroft. (More of him later.) Reverend Flowers laughed and, as I came near, he said, "That's true, Heffernan. Society is bound to buckle, and sooner rather than later. Mankind cannot stand too much unreality."

"Too true," Bancroft said, patting his mouth with a paper napkin, a green palm tree stamped in every corner.

I signaled to Greystone, noticing only then he wore a leather band around his head. For the first time I realized he was an Indian.

"Greystone . . ." I began.

"We are in my home country now, Brown. The masks are off. My true name is Gray Wolf."

"How is the general?"

He raised his eyebrows. Wrinkles rose above them, were stopped by the tight leather band. "He'll hold out for as long as is necessary."

Perhaps the general will be the first old soldier who'll never die, I thought; carried off like Isaiah.

"Jason!" Greystone cried; a command. The blond man came quickly, carrying his shameful smile with him. "Bring this man a ginger ale," Greystone ordered.

"I don't really want a ginger ale," I said.

"Of course you don't, Brown. But the fellow's got to be kept in line. Every order is a test. We'll see if he's got what it takes."

Jason returned with the ginger ale. I thanked him. Greystone scowled. "Run along now, Jason," he said, not unkindly. Reverend Flowers joined us. Putting his mouth behind his hand, he said to Greystone, "That man, Bancroft, has brought those girls here for breeding purposes. This cannot be permitted."

Greystone waved him away. "We are beyond your piddling morality now, Reverend."

"Sir!"

"There are more important matters to hand, Reverend."

"It is *because* of that, Greystone, that I say this. We do not want the grand object of all our strivings to be sullied." He moved away, evidently hurt by Greystone's response.

"0800 hours, Brown. The general will want you then at headquarters. The grotto."

I nodded. He turned on his heel and walked to the bar, pushing Jason rudely aside. Senior, beside me again, said, "He's organizing the Seven Nations. Messengers arrive every day; they have set up an encampment on the south rim."

As I was leaving, tired from the drive and tired of

the noise of this place, Bancroft approached me. "I should like to speak with you, if I may, Dr. Brown."

"Tomorrow," I said, practising Greystone's brusqueness.

He minded it no more than Jason had. "In the afternoon, perhaps? That would be best for me." I agreed and he thanked me. He bade me goodnight and said, "It is good to have men of your calibre here, Doctor."

I walked to my cabin and prepared for sleep. The cabin adjoining mine was dark; we shared a common, shallow porch with two rocking chairs. In the light wind from the desert they rocked gently like small boats at anchor. I undressed in darkness, wanting the view of distance at my window. Standing there I saw Greystone walk up and sit down in the rocker; his weight stopped its movement. Was he looking at the campfires burning on south rim? In their fluttering light I could see the wigwams bulking behind. Fatigue ticked in me but I could not move away from that sight, wanted to fuse with it, take it into myself. Did not notice Jason's approach; saw him only when he was already on the porch and had fallen to his knees in front of Greystone; saw Greystone's dark hand stroking the yellow hair. Jason whispered, "Look, I've brought you this rose." They kissed. Jason flung his head back. "Oh my wild Indian!" he said, his voice trembling. Thin walls of pre-Asia condemned me to witness their love; for hours I was kept awake by the blond man's crying, his moans, his protests. "Oh beast, beast, beast," he whispered. "Oh beast, beast, animal, lover, love me, love me."

twenty-eight

IT COULD ONLY have been Johnson, Jason's former partner in Intelligence. I got out of bed and went to the window; sun assaulted my eyes; Johnson rippled in its waves and seemed to float a few inches above the sand. "Jason," he called, "it's not too late. Come back. I haven't sent in the report yet." He held a bouquet of flowers that were dying in his hand, drooping as I watched.

"Go a-*way!*" Jason shouted; and through the wall I

heard him whisper—I was placed in two worlds at once, an accident of location—to Greystone, "Oh, the evil man!" And Greystone came to the window, invisible to Johnson who had the sun to contend with; to him he must have been only a dark and menacing presence behind the screened window. Greystone's voice was low. "Push off, Johnson," he said, "or I'll cut you down in cold blood." Johnson floated away on the shimmering waves, listing a bit to the left as if he had been badly loaded. He dropped the flowers at the corner post of my little porch, memorial now to some anonymous death.

Jason said, "Was there ever anyone so brave as you! Love, let me do something for you before you go off to your important duties."

"All right," Greystone said. "Do something."

I looked at my watch and began to dress. It was seven o'clock; I'd have coffee and be back at eight for my appointment with the general. Impossible to dress fast enough; had once again to be witness to their love, which sounded like avarice. Greystone said, "In my tribe, in the old days, you'd have been sent off to live with the women."

Jason giggled. "What a terrible fate, lovy. But come here now; I'd like to prove something to my own satisfaction."

I walked to my car; thought of the penny-candy cases in the lounge, full of fraudulent exhibits, of Brice the fox, of Jason and Greystone and their greedy, desperate love. Oddly, this seemed the best thing to have happened thus far; too easy in this sandy place, under palms, to think of those ancient sinful cities blasted by His wrath. No, what bloomed here was a delicious bouquet of farewells; Greystone was saying goodby to earthly pleasures, storing up memories for infinity. Yes, in the imminence of that immensity the Reverend Flowers' morality was indeed piddling. The thought of purity—those perfect realms we were soon to reach—made me lustful; for a moment I thought of turning back, to join those two or, at least, watch them. This imminent and grand departure, it is bound to unsocket us a little, do something to the currents of our desire. (When the day comes for you, friend, I think you'll see what I mean. Get a bottle and a blonde, you think, and wait in pleasure for extinction? And if the blonde turns out to be the husband of your best friend, sir? In the final moment, I suspect, we will reject no one, embrace even the enemy, assaulter, comforter.)

I drove past the Indian encampment; dogs barked and men looked up from their fires. Their wickiups are full of secrets; they know some things (Atlanteans, after all) but they aren't telling. Never mind: in that early morning crystal purity I could smell victory; saw hands reaching out for hands; embraces. Let me spell it out for you, friend: two ways are possible and two only: intervention by Them, or destruction here of all. Only remnants will survive, a few bands of hunters and food gatherers; we will meet on some bleak and blasted plain, former assaulters and assaulted and we'll (as I said above) embrace; because, like bickering ancient husband and wife, we will have been through so much together. And besides, besides, besides, who else will there be who'll take our hands? The others will never trust us again and we'll be left with each other in indefinite togetherness. Cultural exchanges; annual laying of flowers on their dead cities and ours, one for them and one for us. We'll understand each other like Germany and France, because we've *shared*. Jazz for them and balalaikas for us; the advanced among us will take to wearing high-necked blouses and bast shoes, name daughters Natasha, and dream of hot nights in Crimea. We'll be as one (you'll see) and those who dreamed of a governorship and a coach-and-four in Odessa will settle for reading Gogol in Georgetown. In fact, we'll be stuck with each other.

I stopped at the first restaurant on the main street of the town of Twelvepalms, an unplanned gathering of frame houses and stores along the state highway. No railroad station but, as in most such rudimentary places, a small airport baked at the edge of town and a two-motor plane offered passenger service, once a day, to Phoenix. A propeller plane, it had a quaint, antique air; a mechanic wiped it with a dirty cloth, more for encouragement (I thought) than cleanliness.

The restaurant was owned by a Greek, an unlucky people, afflicted from their earliest days with the disease of scientism, their magic long forgotten—if, indeed, they ever had any.

"What'll it be?" the Greek said. The plastic radio, color of gravy, hummed at his elbow; and over all the air-conditioner roared and dripped its captured moisture through a copper pipe onto the gray boards of the porch. I ordered eggs (felt that peculiar American need, *tu sais*) and coffee; and turned to select the table that was waiting for me, and saw Beatrice. She was smiling, waiting to be noticed; surprised, speechless, I stumbled toward her, wondering: Is she one of us? But hardly thought it before rejecting it. Impossible!

"You here?" I said.

"I'm as surprised as you, Bill," she said, and added, archly, "but infinitely more pleased than you seem to be."

"Delighted to see you, Bea, of course."

"You are wondering what I'm doing here in the desert and you are too cautious to ask? Ah, Bill, I promise to take your curiosity as no more than curiosity. You must try sometime not to count the cost with me, Bill."

Impossible. Why was it she always made me feel unreal? Put me at one remove from reality, like an American in an English novel?

She asked what I was doing in Twelvepalms and I told her I was just passing through. "I hope you'll be around for a little while, at least, Bill. I'm sure I shall be lonely. I'm staying here for three weeks; the silly law, you know. For divorce."

"Ah."

"I shall be staying at The Oasis. The Welmor Beauty Ranch, you know?" She smiled, to let me know it was only half a joke. "I shall come out a new woman."

"Regimen of mineral mud baths, unstrenuous exercises, much rest and Ry-Krisps?"

"Actually, it's run along quite scientific lines," she said. "It begins with a thorough physical checkup, to see just how *much* the body can bear."

The Greek brought my eggs, then retired to his nest of coffee urns and plastic surfaces, the materials and objects that give our straggling overextended country a superficial air of continuity.

"Terribly expensive, of course," she said. "It was a gift from Mother who thought my heart was broken." She raised her chin, bravely and proudly. No, you see, the thing I have against her is that it's really impossible—I mean, really, it is—impossible even to speak of her without falling into ladies'-magazine prose. *Bravely and proudly!* Faugh! Oh she wanted everyone's stamp of approval, this one did; she wanted everything *kitchen-*

tested; she read the testimonials before using. Live dangerously? She'd rather die.

"And guess what," she said. "Do you know who's going to be staying there the last two weeks of my stay? —The wife of the Secretary of Defense."

"Yes, I believe I read that."

"I am told she swears by it."

"It has done wonders for her, I suppose?"

"Well," Beatrice said, "she *is* remarkably well preserved."

(*Preserved!* Trust Bea to use such a word and mean it as a desirable condition! I had an immediate vision of foetuses in jars.)

The Beauty Ranch station wagon sounded its horn and Bea stood up. She was wearing slacks; we said good-by and I promised to come see her. "Any time after seven in the evening, Bill. Those are the Relaxation hours." The porch boards sagged and clattered as she made her way to the car; of course, being in the West, she was wearing boots; of course. The Greek, leaning on his classical ho ho elbow, watched her and pulled his lower lip. "I see them come," he said, "and I see them go." This represents, I am bound to say, no degeneration of the philosophy of his forebears; both were merely responding to observed reality, poor souls, Heraclitus, Plato, Socrates, and this counterman. It's all one: a steady line, diminishing strength; by such means has the power of this planet been drained. We are *preserved* in that classical dry death-giving air, have made of this world a disorderly museum. Certain forces still remain to be unleashed.

twenty-nine

BEHIND THE ALTAR in the grotto, a door (Protestant's dream of sinister Catholic mysteries): the general's HQ. Not a big room, at first sight, but then one saw that it extended deep into the earth beyond the lighted area. The light, its edges cut off sharp, made a small square room within the vastness of the cavern. On an easel there was hung a map of the world—signifying Ambition; another was spread over the top of a table, signifying nothing at all unless it was the normal redundancy of the military. There was also a blackboard and, printed there in yellow chalk, the words OPERATION NOTORIETY. Familiar feel of grittiness in the air; product of a powerful remorse; and of panic, of course.

Greystone bolted the door behind us. The general and another man sat in canvas campaign chairs; mouths pursed, eyes identically narrowed, they studied the map of the world, traced Ambition's contours, sought to locate and mark it on the grid. "Billy," the general said, "we are surrounded." Then he stood up, no small effort for him, shook hands with me, and introduced the other man: Tom Ironsides, the retired admiral Santander had mentioned. The admiral's hair was paper-white, so neat it looked like a wig; and he had the round innocent eyes of a well-fed and dearly loved boy. "Welcome aboard, Brown," he said.

"We're surrounded, Bill." Backhand, with his left arm, the general made a magician's sweeping gesture toward the map. I expected it then to disappear, or twelve birds to fly out with little American flags between their beaks. I was ready to applaud; I held myself ready.

"Look at the red area, Bill; a spreading cancer. Brave little Finland, brave little Belgium and Luxembourg, brave West Germany; yes, a few islands of resistance remain, that is all."

"They provide footholds," the admiral said. "Stepping-stones to Final Victory."

"Yes, Tom, they do," the general said.

"And I'd like to point out, general, that the ocean seas are still blue."

"True enough, true enough. Oh, I don't say we're defeated; I don't say that. But we've got our backs to the wall."

"We're still mobile, general."

"We are far from lost," the general said. "Far from it. I'm not, God knows, one of your defeatists. As you know, admiral, I am not one of those with the will to lose."

"Thank God for that, general. Every day I thank God for that."

The general sat down; he seemed to be resting his tired arms on the arms of the chair; shoulders sagged and his melting head seemed too much for him; he let it drop forward. He said, "I used to think we could always count on the Swedes, but . . ."

The admiral laughed. "Not a chance. It's a soft country. I understand, what's more, that their ball bearings are not what they used to be."

"Is that so?" the general said. "Well, that's a point in our favor, isn't it?"

Something (hairy and rutting) moved in the darkness, beyond the area of light, at the back of the cavern; I knew it at once for what it was, had not a moment's doubt, will not hesitate to name it: Violence. Would know it anywhere, its peculiar odor and gestuary. Born and raised in this unfinished wild country it is my familiar, brother; have known it from childhood: underside of our well-known get-up-and-go, the old vinegar, sauce, moxie, that pep, vim and vigor we've heard so much about. Saw them again those wandering bands dressed any old which way, eating seeds and berries. We are moving that way, friend, pellmell, hell for leather, *comme on dit.* Frightened survivors, a pale people who travel only by night, will see us coming and cry the warning: *Russkys!* And we will call out to them: *No, no, Americans!* No matter; they'll run, anyway, just as frightened. Oh we're making a name for ourselves, aren't we? Friend, we've got the power to break the arches of the earth and don't you forget it.

They were lost in the map, the two old men, seeking their perfect lat. and long., confluence of Lust and Violence, there where Ambition has its source and bubbles up from a crack between two ordinary-seeming rocks. Ironsides roused himself from dream of discovery and said, slapping the arm of his chair, "Give me six ships, general, and I'll hand you West Europe on a platter. I happen to know the French will scuttle their fleet again, and the Italians don't worry me at all. An overcivilized people, they haven't got the will to win."

"What about England?"

Ironsides shrugged. "England will be bypassed. It's no loss, either way."

"Oh, I agree with you there, Tom, I agree with you there. We don't need it."

"It's now an unnecessary country. Best forgotten, I think. Well, you know, general, they've written it off themselves. They mustn't take on because others do."

"Bill!" The general turned to me, swung round in his chair, a galvanic movement. "Bill, we've got to bring this home to the people, get our message across to them. We've got no radio station or TV outlet, we don't own a newspaper. But we've got to *use* them, these means of communicating. An action that will make headlines, Bill, that's what's wanted and that's what we've devised." He pointed to the blackboard: OPERATION NOTORIETY.

The admiral was still staring at the map of the world. "Can Franco be trusted?" he asked. "What about Salazar? Are they Jesuits or are they Christians? That's the sixty-four-dollar question." His forehead showed lines of anguish: thinking's not easy, friend; ask anyone who's tried, I mean really tried. The admiral, at all times, kept a small smile on his face; it was a nervous habit, merely, but it gave a cynical cast to everything he said. Nothing could have been farther from the truth; the poor man was a believer; he suffered from it like a haemophiliac and any touch was sufficient to start him bleeding. Under his old dress uniform beat a cranky heart; and under his hat—that curved, frilled thing like an upside-down gondola—what dreams, images, ambitions were stored. Against the grotto's damp he wore a cape, gold rippling on the high up-standing collar. He had the easy manner of an old man whose pension is more than adequate; knows he can spend the cold winter in any incredible Florida he has a mind to.

The general tapped the map with his forefinger, that hand now an incomplete fist, but fanged and more powerful than ever. Finger tapping map: it is one of the elementary gestures of violence, along with hands on hips, along with legs spread wide and finger pointing toward horizon. Oh the invisible worm that attacked poor Rose was present in this cave; I could feel it working at the sheath of my heart. Here behind the altar the spirit of man was being betrayed and the hunger for destruction elaborated. We are back at the beginning of history, friend, aren't we? Ironside's teeth glistened as he bent forward. "That's it," he said.

"Right here, Billy boy," the general said, his finger tapping where two red arteries crossed, a place without a name, "right here's the spot, soft and unprotected, that'll be Their undoing. And the making of us. Oh, there'll be hell to pay."

"What is it?" I asked.

"A powerhouse."

"A powerhouse," Ironsides added, "that powers the whole damn early warning defense system."

"Knock it out, Bill, and you've dealt a crippling blow."

"And won fame for our cause," Ironsides said, smiling. "On the morning after we shall be the living center of a great rally of the American people. We will be the light that opens their eyes to the truth."

"And more than that, Bill," the general said. "More than that. They're trying to give away the early warning defense system; those people down in Washington have offered to hook it up with the Russky system. Oh they're giving it all away—the transatlantic cable is being handed to them on a platter, too, you know—and they've got to be stopped. We must let the people know, Bill, and we'll do it in one blow and grab every headline in the land and all the prime time TV has to offer. They'll be *made* to listen."

"To say nothing of the woman."

The general smiled; he was pleased but tried hard to be modest. "Just a peripheral thing, a little insurance, Bill; something for the tabloids, to titillate the masses. At that so-called Beauty Ranch down the road a piece—you've heard of it?—the wife of the Secretary of Defense is getting an overhauling."

Ironsides laughed. "Annual checkup," he said, "change of oil."

"We intend to kidnap her," the general said.

"Well, not really kidnap, general."

"Greystone's men will carry her off—kidnaping is of course the wrong word for it, it isn't kidnaping at all—no question of ransom. She'll be held for long enough to make headlines, and then released."

I said nothing!

The general was silent a moment; then he turned away from me and (this must be said for him) said, "Well, we none of us like it, Billy, but it must be done. Military necessity."

"Must make use of every tool that presents itself to us," Ironsides said. Not apologetic at all, arrogant and smug, the tarnished gold of his collar catching the light, sending out its pathetic signals, trivial last gasps of a man with a head full of treacle. Too long on the bridge and hypnotized by his Annapolis ring; product of a flawed education and (trouble with all the military) an overprotected life.

The general stared at the map, waited for it to come to life and provide him with a small-screen preview of the great event. He said, "And on the next day, Bill—of course we won't be here to see it, but sure as God made apples, Bill, on the next day there will be an alerted America, an America in arms."

"We'll be a million miles away by then," the admiral said, his voice full of longing.

"We will return, Ironsides."

"We will, indeed, general; of course we will."

I looked at the map: red lines for disaster, blue for despair; no cartilage area here, only emptiness, a waste of secondary roads, desert, and one small pocket of hope to make any risk worth the taking. I wanted to scratch myself; grittiness had laid its fine deposit on my skin; I shivered in my clothes, hunched myself and made them a tent around me and heard the banner at the tent's peak crack in the wind.

The beast hunched and rubbed its back against the grotto's rough walls, there in the cavernous dark. So much terror abroad in the land, so much of it there must be in order to light the fire of violence in these tired old hearts, eh? I felt myself thrilling to it! Felt its force between my shoulderblades! Oh we must all be on guard, we who live in a time when to praise violence is a sign of virtue. We've been terrorized by the immoral; the soul is prey to fungus and the worm; it secretes a terrible liqueur.

"We need your help, Billy," the general said.

"I'm at your service, sir," I said—in so deep the response was automatic, conditioned by my whole life's way; and though the heart cries, aghast, we obey the snapped command, hear the trumpets, see the flags break and tatter in the iron wind of will. Like Aristotle's good ho ho soldier, we obey: obedient and *good* we kill, go mad, betray humanity (our first loyalty and therefore always the first to be betrayed).

Half an hour later, rolled map in hand, diploma of that awful school, I walked out into the sunlight of the old world, a graduate now, an alumnus, booster, traveler to homecoming games, friend of the coach. All I needed now was dentures, sure sign the soul's been sold down-river (isn't it?).

Walked to my cabin and spread out the map, anchoring it on one side with a volume of Rimbaud, Rilke on the other, and sat down to my task. Slide-rule warrior, most bloodthirsty of them all. Sick, I laid my forehead on the table and prayed that They would come.

Come now, I prayed, now, come now and save us all. Oh divine, healing, perfect, come at once and lead us, the chosen, away from here that we might preserve our few and precious seeds. Finish us, oh finish us who are so unfinished.

thirty

MY HAND is afflicted with a mind of its own. (We've noted this before, haven't we?) Engaged in an uncongenial task its movements become sluggish; and objects —pencils, pen, ruler—turn reluctant in its grip, catching the contagious Uncaring. I turned scale to miles and converted the powerhouse into so many cubes, the cubes to necessary pounds of dynamite; and marked rendezvous points for before and after. Greystone and his Indians, on horse, would meet them *here;* the advance; the attack; and then, then we shall make our perfect getaway. Later, the woman would be released; but that was not part of my problem. I was concerned only with the blowing up of the powerhouse. A simple task. One sheet of paper contained the entire plan of action. And I? What else? I'll go along and watch from a safe distance: what warriors of my sort are expected to do. We'll dirty, not bloody, our hands.

Good soldiers, we go when we're summoned by country or (same thing, really) research foundation ho ho—we go as far as the first desk in the deepest shelter. Precious beings, we'll be preserved, like it or not; they're determined, it seems, to show us the fruit of our handiwork. We'll have our reward: that view of things, that gorgeous harvest our lust long ago sowed, as soon as the earth has cooled sufficiently to be walked on. Then, under asbestos hoods we'll walk on lead-soled shoes, stiff-legged, tottering like learners, Frankenstein and monster both, to see the sights. How strangely beautiful the sky! we'll cry (like tourists face to face with the new). See the sun unfolding! What vistas—how grand, how immense, now that dirty city and flawed suburbs are gone! (All our city-planners' dreams come true: Now we can start from scratch!)

And so we will, from very beginnings: wanderers with half a mind carrying vague recollections of an imperfect, unfinished civilization. I want an end of it all; I want to have no part in *that;* I made my small renunciation (remember, in that other place, a continent away?) and now, betrayer, prepared these marching orders for the general and his followers, and for me: a farewell missal to earth the beloved—left pinned to her pillow and signed with my names: *Coward & Bolter*. Darling, I'm taking a powder, giving up your delicious embrace to push my way into that ship with the general, Ironsides, Senior and those others who want immortality without the desperate fuss of dying.

God knows I understand the terrible desperation that moves them. Who would not? And didn't I (like you, friend, just as you) snap to attention at the general's command? I did. It's so hard to step out of the skins our ways have grown for us. If it's new men we want we shall just have to wait for them. The Hero is the rarest of birds. But I shall be one of them yet, shall return feathered with secrets, the saving knowledge held close to my chest: winning hand. I'm even now preparing myself for adoration, secular certainly but no less intense for that.

I lay down on my bed and stared at the ceiling, grateful for the silence behind the wall. Greystone and his dimpled darling must have been elsewhere or sleeping at last through the hot part of the day. I sat up, startled by the sound of drumming, a muffled roar; then, the cries of men. It was Greystone and his Indians, on their streaming horses, galloping up and down the hard-topped road. Holding spears they warbled war cries and whipped their horses toward Johnson, tied to a post, the Intelligence man, threatened him with lances; but pulled back every time, laughing at him. After a time one of the braves cut the ropes and, taking Johnson by the hair, dragged him to the encampment. Jason rode among them, naked to the waist, red and blue lines painted on his face. I envied him his masquerade.

I ached with homesickness; it was one of those days: I felt the call and pull of home, an awful yearning for the heavenly, perfect place that saw the origins of our birth. I turned on the tape recorder and listened once again to the voices calling. Hideous not to be able to understand: my own family, my first language, those voices ululating from the cradle of the human race. I felt the marvelous tidal tug. One more secret unfolded and I shall be able to cut loose the web of earth and achieve that perfect world, I know it, I know it. I rocked to the rhythm of those voices, that delicious choral. *Brüder!* Soon we shall embrace!

Hearing footsteps on the porch I switched off the machine; for some reason—perhaps recalling her boots on the porch of the luncheonette—I thought it was Beatrice come to see me and felt a prickling sensation (quite unwilled, I assure you) in my loins. It was Bancroft; I had forgot my appointment with him.

Even wearing a sport shirt, tieless, he looked like a businessman; no mask can disguise them, they have a giveaway aura, permanently there. They are born with it. He wore sporty striped cotton trousers and black shoes and gunmetal lisle socks with clocks. Clipped to his belt was a plastic holster containing three ball-point pens. No more than fifty, yet his gross molecules had betrayed him: his belly sagged into his lap like a bundle of laundry, his hair was thin and revealed a scalp the color of his socks.

Bancroft talked; he spun circles around his object, touched it lightly and spiraled away again, followed (I was certain) the rules laid down in a book written years ago by a successful drummer, and advertised as The Salesman's Bible. I rested through all this, listened with half an ear, knew I'd know when he came to the point. "What I like to call *donors,*" he said. "It's donors I need and I don't have to tell you, doctor, they don't grow on trees. A handful at the most, to begin with; then, after my rigorous tests—a thorough weeding-out process, let me tell you—I may be left with one or two donors. Sometimes, in some groups, I end with none. I can't be too careful. One bad product, one unsatisfied customer, and I'm finished. Then I'd be just like the others, running up to Canada and picking them up where I can, not inquiring into antecedents, just accepting the first healthy baby offered and selling it to just anyone. I am, you might say, engaged in the carriage trade; it's a quality operation, if I do say so myself. I have contacts on every major campus in the country and a waiting list of over a hundred couples. And, mind you, doctor, I accept no one under the rank of associate professor. If I accepted assistants and lecturers—well, it would get out of hand completely. This is the kind of operation where, once you go into mass production, you've had it, you've lost it all. The academic community would cease to have the confidence in me that I now enjoy." He offered me a cigar; I declined; he put it back in its plastic holster.

"I have twelve women, doctor. All have been very carefully, very rigorously, selected. None are over twenty-five years of age; all have an IQ of 140 or over; all are of sound stock and have been investigated three generations back for any sign of mental or physical instability. I have just delivered twelve new infants to their new parents—five to Ivy League colleges, four to Big Ten faculty, and three in the California system. As of this year, seventy-two of my products are growing up in the academic atmosphere. Group One is now six years old; they are in the first grade and all of them are in the upper one-tenth of their class. That, I might tell you, is a record that's hard to beat."

"Why do you limit yourself to the academic community?" I asked, more out of politeness—showing an Interest, *tu sais*—than any genuine curiosity.

Bancroft smiled. "I thought you would ask that," he said, following the rules of his Bible: Make the Client feel Important. "Yes, well, it all started quite by chance with a professor at Berkeley; he came to me in some distress and I began to look into the matter. I was shocked to discover the high incidence of sterility and barrenness among faculty circles, and determined then and there to do something about it. These people, our best minds, mind you, doctor, had to be provided with issue; it is necessary, it is vital if our intellectual life is to have continuity. After all, let's face it, doctor, you are special people. I divide mankind into ten classes; I won't bother you with the breakdown now but it will suffice, I think, if

I put it in the form of a question: Is the attendant at your favorite gasoline station a man like Beethoven or Aristotle? Of course he is not; he is not. There are giants, doctor, men who tower over their contemporaries; they are special, they are mutants. I have no doubt the time will come when science will be able to plan the alteration of heritable human traits by artificially induced mutations. But, until that time comes, we will just have to do the best we can with selective pairing, as I call it.

"Doctor Brown, I know and you know of the holocaust to come. I know and you know of the black wave that towers over us. We must prepare against that day. We must provide the human race with a cadre of physically hardy and intellectually superior children, souls fit to survive and with the capacity to survive. They will be the inheritors, walking treasure chests of our civilization, guarantors of the future, builders of the new world out of the smoking embers of the old. I know you, doctor. In my business I've come across many like you in my travels to and fro from one campus to another across the breadth of this land. I know you and I know, therefore, that your first loyalty is to the race."

And to this apple world.

"Can I count on your cooperation, doctor?"

"As a donor?"

"As a donor." He waited for me to speak; he had let a fly into my cabin and it whirred from wall to wall; there was the sound of drumming now from south rim. Then he said, "There so few real men any more." Something so wistful and pained in his voice; I was moved by it. I agreed. He offered to let me choose any one of the three he had brought with him. "I'll walk them by your window and, later, you can tell me which you want." He insisted on shaking hands. He congratulated me. "You should have sons everywhere," he said.

"Just one, Bancroft."

"All right, just one, doctor. I won't insist. You're doing your duty. This is one act you'll never regret." At the door he paused and said, "From this day forward, Dr. Brown, you will never be alone."

He put his hand on my shoulder, lightly; it was an award, he knighted me, made me part of the brotherhood. My knees trembled; I was overcome with weakness. I sat at the window and waited for him to return with the girls. He walked them past me and I chose the one in the middle: dark skin, fair hair, her mouth lightly touched with pink lipstick. He came to the screen door and I told him my choice. "I'll send her tonight," he said. "No, now!" He ran across the sand and I watched her turn and walk toward my cabin, breaking through the oily heat waves, at times seeming to float. I opened the door for her. She embraced and undressed me, then lay down beside me; I touched her milky breasts. "This will be my fourth," she said. "I've always conceived in love. I love you."

I was seized with revulsion, wanted no part of this. That cocoon I had dreamed in Wunter enwrapt me again, that fragile filament would protect me from her and her employer's scientism, this armor would save me. She grappled me, heel and palm. She kissed my mouth. I laughed inwardly and thought to myself: she'll get nowhere. But *she,* she moved and by some stratagem broke through my sheath. Her hooked forefinger found the way to open me! There was some crevice she had the clue to. Like the elders of Wunter that woman chopped down my tree, opened me to progress and diversified industries; then rested there, her body touching mine. I slept. Like a cat she sat and watched me, basalt, tight-skinned, Pharaonic; I felt the grand stone-block weight of pyramid over me. She licked my eyelids and I awoke. "It's now or never," she said, and undid my sheath once more, sweet filament, came in to the tent and shared with me. "Prodigy!" she said, and clamped me in iron, scissored; bent and broke me again.

At nightfall, when the fires of the Indians became visible against the sky, she left me. "I keep strict hours," she said, "and never eat white bread." At the door I knelt and kissed her hands and thighs; she was sacred now.

thirty-one

I HAD NOTHING now but time; could indulge myself in anything while waiting for The Last Day, that dawn two nights away when the general and Ironsides would drive to the powerhouse in the army-surplus halftrack purchased with their retirement pay in some secondhand-car lot in Tucson and rendezvous with painted Indians (what madness) but also with *Them*. That moment will mark the turnabout of all things; lambs and ploughshares at last and an end of mere talk.

But I wanted her back. Half an hour after she had gone I wanted her back, that milky girl; I thought I'd like to keep and grapple her for nine more months, then watch her produce my son in blood. I'd take him away, tucked under my arm like someting casual, a hat or a map—to fool the jealous gods, *tu sais*—and leave her to be covered by another, which is what she wants, ideal new woman. Then I'd take my darling boy and raise him on berries, stone-ground flour, grand visions, and Daddy's high ideals, and Daddy's incomparable mission. Hi ho but it was not to be. In the morning I sought Bancroft out, found him, and said, "Look here, Bancroft, I want her again." Sent her back, he said; he had already sent her back, her duty done. "But don't fret, Doctor Brown," he said, "I have two others." I thanked him and walked away, turned my back on him once and for all. Only the fair-haired one would do for we had already made a child in love; and I could not, not on such short order, love again. I need a little more time than that. Well, it's laughable, isn't it? I mean, really I am more concerned with standards than is Bancroft. On second thought, though the business is his, this is not too surprising: *because* the business is his, don't you see, friend. God save us from the petite bourgeoisie, eh? Rather the really powerful in their furs and uniforms. Yes, yes, I know, friend, this has all got to do with the first desk in the deepest shelter: just as every Frenchman during the Occupation had his Jew, so now every one of us wants his general. Khaki priests, they assure us a place on earth, to keep us dry when the great wave crashes, or a seat on the ship that will carry us to perfect safety in elsewhere. They are the new sellers of indulgences and we pay through the nose, don't we?

But all that was next morning and by the by. Meanwhile there was a night to be got through. For a while I was content to lie on my bed in the odor of her fertility (a simple compound of farina and cinnamon), but then I wanted coffee (don't laugh, friend, it's the only elixir we've got) and walked to the lounge. I could see its lights from my porch and walked toward it across the white sands. In the moonlight all was brazenly clear: every crack and fishy scale in the sunblasted paint of the cabin walls, and the crossed fingers of the tentpoles rising through the wigwams' apices on south rim. Dogs barked there, disturbed by my passage. Johnson was tied to a post and slept sitting, chin on chest, crying in his sleep. (Oh how easily mortified they are, like those poor Japanese tennis players who—before the war, remember?—were always committing suicide, unable to face the folks back home because they lost, 6-4, 6-3, 6-3. This should be a lesson to us all: failure makes them dangerous and, if we were truly wise, we'd pray they might have a few measly successes, to keep them going, *tu sais,* to keep them from turning on themselves and us in their terrible desperation. Lacking a ruling idea they lurch toward chaos, the only solution they know. Recall, I beg you, Herostratus who burned down the temple of Artemis [small potatoes, eh?—But then, it was a smaller world] to make his name immortal. One thing more: Beware the leader who has *a sense of history.* He'll set the world on fire for mention in a footnote in the final, definitive work. Don't say I didn't warn you, friend.)

In the lounge: behind the soda bar, Brice's wife, aproned and motherly, counted nickels into columns of twenty, an easy way to make a dollar. I ordered coffee and carried it to the table where Greely, Sr., beckoned me and called. He sat with a tow-headed boy who wore a T-shirt and had the sterile muscled health of a lifeguard; what little manhood he had was trapped forever, willing prisoner, in his jockstrap. It was young Heffernan; I should have known. Senior introduced him: "Grandson of the man who was my undoing." Senior's cup was afloat in a saucer of coffee: sign of age. "Billy," he said, "we have been discussing the mercury problem. Young Heffernan here thinks he's on the verge of breaking it."

"Well, I do think it's just a matter of time," the boy said with beginner's confidence. He approached mercury as if it were a flivver; he *tinkered* with it, the old American itch, *tu sais.* "We know that power is there," he said, portentous as a vice president.

"It's just a matter of finding the trigger," Senior said.

"It's just a matter of releasing the power, then containing and controlling it," Heffernan said, making his minor amendment, a big-deal kid.

Really I should have found it amusing the way he talked of mercury; but I could not. Perhaps should not. After all, he was speaking of that water which is at the same time fire. He knew nothing, clearly he knew nothing of the alchemists' description of mercury. I could have told this boy—but did not—I could have told him of their Mercurius *hermaphroditus* and *duplex,* the Gods' messenger, One and All. But held my tongue. Such knowledge is for myself alone now; I decided this then and there. I decided to husband and turn it to account for the world's sake, not Heffernan's. It is *not* for him! I let him talk and held my tongue; he rambled on, articulate, brainless hobbyist without knowledge, unread and unenlightened; he had only a few tags of learning and made the most of them. Senior nodded, enjoyed his elder statesman's role, the boy's respectful sir-ing of him, the delicious knowing that here in his palm, in his camp, was the grandson of Professor Heffernan, who had scourged him in Pittsburgh in the old days.

I sat between them there at the table but they were less important to me than the desert at my back. I adored its silence, its vastness, its way of being both beautiful and harsh; and how it withheld itself, kept its essence a secret tight as a bud. What did not move at its center, at night, in broad day, even? Saw myself there, at the center; in deep, yet fearless and at ease, knowing my power to tap water from the rock. Yes, friend, yes, yes, at such a time as this, when the world is rent and the split appears, a savior is a necessity. Unwilled he will come forth; almost, as it were, an act of nature, product of the split, what rushes in when the vacuum is created. He is the saving force disaster elaborates. Tension manifests itself in energy. Remember this.

Heffernan, poor tow-head boy: he has never heard of Hermes *katachthonios,* the subterranean Mercurius, bright and burning-hot spirit; great magician; he who can dissolve and bind, both. (I do not say I have that power. *I do not say it!*)

"Mercury was the water of the Philosophers," Senior said, "used to transmute and transform. As we all know."

"That's right, sir," the boy said.

And known also (I could have told them) as *servator mundi,* preserver of the world. I closed my eyes at the thought of it. Let them do what they will with me, I said, I shall save them in spite of themselves. Mercurius: healer, peacemaker, springing fountain, Gideon's dew; I know myself now, and what my real name is. Was it possible that my radiance did not blind these two? I gourmandized on the superessential bread; my spiritual hunger knew feasting at last, there at that unlikely table.

"Don't fall asleep, Billy," Senior said. "The Sunrise Service commences soon at the grotto."

"I'll meet you there," I said or believe I said; and went out of that place of nickels and dimes to watch dawn curdle the sky.

They are split in two as the world is, I thought, Heffernan and Senior and all the rest. Only I am whole.

thirty-two

I SLEPT THE day away and woke at dusk; I had dreamt of Mary Kovarchuk yet my first waking thought was of the fair-haired girl, her odor of farina still on me. But she was gone: therefore I thought of Beatrice, nearby and available. How marvelous to live in advanced countries; we don't have to run to whores, we've got the ex-wives of friends. But I rejected even the thought of her. Besides, there would be other, more important, actions at the Beauty Ranch tonight; and besides, by now her breath must smell of carrot juice, and her skin (overlaying the suburban grubbiness, the enlarged pores of pre-Asia) would be pearly with an altogether artificial purity: compound of wax, medicinal mud, unspeakable unguents. Shrugged off the consequent feelings of guilt; because, you understand, I could have saved her, could have taught her to abstain from that no life at all, which is their way of preparing us for no life at all. I left the cabin without washing my face; not because of any need for haste—no, it was for myself, sign of my uncaring. I had made my farewell, was done with flesh, had with the milky girl my last night before the daybreak that will bring the true passion.

In the camp all was waiting; time stood like a stalled horse. Soon now the Indians' departure would put spurs to it; then all will be resolved in the madness of action.

To think of it quickened the blood. From the porch of my cabin I could see Greystone and his men packing the crates of dynamite in the back of the command car, khaki chariot for the Emperor of the Last Days. And would he, like the *pauperes,* be found at Jerusalem's walls with the sign of mercury between his shoulder blades? We will see. Of myself I have no doubts: at my table, I am certain, the food will increase as it is eaten.

On the porch, on a rocking chair, I sat and watched the others bring the plan to life. Fires extinguished now on south rim, long ropes of smoke seemed permanently to stand against the luminous sky, plated by moonlight. I looked at my watch, thought of my son. Think of it, friend, in nine months he will be among you; by the time you read this he is there. You, reader, somewhere on your Big Ten campus, does your heart beat faster at the thought that the boy reading in his favorite armchair, that child you call your own, may be mine? Look at him bent over his homework or his stamps. He does not hear you when you call and looks up, at last, and looks at you with another's eyes. Does he take long walks alone? Has a strongbox and keeps the key hidden? Did he examine his own blood under his first microscope? Does complicated sums in his head? Collects odd-shaped stones? Experiments with iodine on a lump of coal? Seems able to communicate with lizards and hamsters? Clever at card tricks, makes the jacks disappear? Dear reader, he is mine!

Full night; the stripes of smoke no longer visible. Stars appear as on a screen within the brackets of my vision. I searched among them for that one which moved with a will of its own; imagined myself on that craft, assessing earth's curvature, watching the continents emerge from cloud cover, observing conjecture's conversion to reality, setting the course for Twelvepalms. Reverend Flowers put his elbow on the railing of my little porch; for a moment, together, we watched the activity in the Indian camp: saddling of horses, dogs rolling in furry packs. He said, "You did not come to me for the church's blessing." And when I did not answer, he said, "Nothing personal, of course."

Silence again. Dogs barked. There was activity, a sound like that made by a man who takes a new position in his sleep. "I have been thinking of death," Reverend Flowers said.

In their long saddle-holsters the butts of the Indian rifles were sparked by moonlight, puddles of silver against dark flanks, black manes; only light there was on south rim, metal's glimmer among dark skins.

"Is a good death possible?" Reverend Flowers asked. "Any longer, these days? I have been wondering. I don't except myself, Brown. I number myself among you and don't stand apart because of my calling. Like you I am a victim of subliminal urgings. I fear operations. What if, under anaesthesia, I should say: *Mother, please, I'd rather do it myself!* Or some other TV commercial that has wormed its way and made a home for itself in my head? Brother, I would be ashamed."

Two men carrying a five-gallon can began to fill the tanks of those cars that would be used in the expedition. They approached my Plymouth.

"Or worse," Flowers said. "What if in the moment of total and lovely repose at the coffin's very edge, some steel-voiced white-toothed announcer should cry: *You're on camera!*—Oh God, how awful if we should open our eyes and respond! Brother, it's going to be very, very difficult to make a good death. The sensitive among us—men like you and me, Brown—will be too tense. I know it, I know it. We'll cross over with our mouths clamped shut, no consoling words for the living will pass our lips. We'll breathe our last through our noses like three New York doctors out of five."

Greystone was horsed; he carried a lance with leather thongs, the shaft painted red and black: bad medicine sign. He'd leave it for marker and declaration. The small troop cantered past the cabins; war-paint shone like sweat, as if it had not been applied but had oozed from their pores. Hoofs were nearly silent in the sand, a hissing sound; and when they struck the highway it was a sudden tattoo and diminished swiftly in distance.

"It begins," Flowers said. He sighed. He had tried to do his best for me; I could almost hear him saying it to himself. Not willing to accept his blessing, I was to have my thoughts turned toward death; rejecting him, I must prepare myself. Well, I felt kindly toward him, a mistaken but a not ungenerous man; I think we may grant him that. But I needed nothing he had to offer; I was ready, knew myself, had feasted at that banquet where the food never becomes less. He offered his hand and I accepted it; we were of the hidden, final, holy people, were we not? Not embracing him, still there was no cause to reject him.

He went off to the lounge, where they were gathering now, those who would follow the general. Phase Two was to begin in three hours, at midnight. An hour later I would follow, observer and last resort. And at dawn the dynamite will roar like a lion and mystery begin.

I searched the heavens; I wanted to be the first to sight the new land and win the coin that dazzled on the mast. Could Their excitement now at this moment be any less than mine? Surely not, I saw Their leader's hand tremble on the lever as our darling earth tilted and loomed on the screen. Then the three flares, snaky and golden, exploded against the sky, and there was the sudden appearance of many men from the cabins and the lounge. Phase One was under way; the flares announced it; the woman had been kidnaped; the Indians galloped now toward the rendezvous with their notorious prize.

thirty-three

THE NIGHT, unfortunate traveler, moved toward its destination, a peaceful process seen from my vantage on the porch. Dynamite slept in sawdust in the back of the halftrack; the war sign had been struck in the courtyard of the beauty ranch; and the Indians, with their burden of bitterness, bad memories, and hope of dawn's gift, advanced across the desert. By my reckoning they would soon come to the terrace butte, crenelated by weather, pass through its shadow and in the distance see the powerhouse, a concrete cube squatting on the flat horizon. In the camp, there is the peculiar silence made by men waiting, the hush that comes in the wake of grand decisions, all sounds banished from the furrow power has made.

No sign of Them.

No, I do not doubt They will come. How can I? They sleep in me as Charlemagne did in his tomb in Aachen.

Give it time, friend, only give it time: the prayers of man will bring Them forth.

My eyes scanning the heavens I rocked and waited and my palms did not sweat; nor did I start when the halftrack's motor turned over and a loose armored plate clattered, cracked the desert's frozen silence and hurried the men from their cabins. It was the boom of the long winter's breaking, that nearly eternal winter of our waiting. A flock of birds, a sudden respiration of wings, birds that had been sleeping on a bush, took flight, whirred away like fireworks, a celebration of our intentions, salute.

A dun-colored quarter-ton truck ground into line behind the halftrack, sprayed sand from its wheels in its eagerness to be unleashed and gone. In the command car's back seat the general and Ironsides sat, their feet up, resting on the boxes of dynamite. (Slight change of plan here, I noted. There was space enough in the trunk for the explosives.) Ironsides, flamboyant in his admiral's cape and the gold rippling dully on his collar and cap, waved at (I'm sure he saw them) the throng of thousands ho ho who lined the route, felt the ticker tape's rich tribute on his shoulders, confetti's grace, adulation palpable as epaulets. Had a look of youth on his face: was dreaming now (I'm certain) of old days when he sailed under canvas in the creaking training ship, Nike firm-breasted and gaudy on the prow.

The general, his face held together by will alone—the melting of his head arrested, perhaps, by the coolness of dawn—had his arms crossed, cradling his body which swayed and rocked, never resisted the car's fidelity to earth's delicious contours, its marvelous vagaries. He had the grim look of a dedicated man at the moment of folly. Types like us can't be sporting about defeat, retirement, death. A touch of hope on our nerve ends and we'll be galvanized to action and rise from our coffins; we're like those nobles Saint-Simon wrote about: they took their cancers and last breaths to the grand balls and died handing over their partner in a gavotte. Better that way, eh, friend? Better than to be pampered to death with drugs and the dry hands of doctors. Let's practise this gallantry and forget about the fear of TV commercials; never mind last words, let's die without a breath to spare.

The two cars bucked and tilted as they rose to the concrete highway, then settled on its hardness and soon disappeared in darkness and at the prescribed speed. I went into my cabin and packed my bag, the work of minutes; and when I heard the sharp *thack, thack* of the clasps of the suitcase I knew my farewells were truly made. I'd have no need of these things where I was going; it was habit moved me. I thought only of destination and mechanically performed the old ritual of departure, so meaningless now. Threw the bag in the back seat of my Plymouth and went to the lounge for coffee. Yes, one last hour in the last days of Arizona and I'd spend it that way, at a plastic table drinking only passable coffee. In this desert, what else is provided? We shall have to find our music in another place.

I walked across the sand in the tire-prints of the caravan that lumbered now toward our destiny. The wigwams were gone; south rim was desolate and the wind that precedes dawn here had already obliterated every mark of the camp. I saw Mrs. Brice walking toward the lounge, the only sign of life; and when I had stood for a moment on my porch I heard Johnson snoring on Greystone and Jason's bed. They had drugged him; he would sleep all day. Had he thought it was a lover's potion they were offering him? He drank of it eagerly, in any case, and asked for more. I looked in at him; his face was anguished, consciousness of betrayal informed his restiveness; dutifully he struggled to wake. His snores shamed the hero who slept in him, poor man.

Dull and gray, Mrs. Brice's face had not yet had time to assume its professional look. Her greeting was merely dutiful; I did not mind; I took my coffee and sat at the window, glanced at my watch and, on the map spread in my mind, located them, a third of the way to the rendezvous, passing now the abandoned mine and the shack where the Indians had left the wife of the Secretary of Defense. Raising the cup to my lips I saw the airport taxi emerge from the mint-green dawn, watched it turn off the highway and drive up to the lounge. Greely, Jr., stepped out. I rapped on the window; he turned and, not surprised to see me, paid off the driver and entered the lounge. His face white, he looked more than ever like a bank teller; but a harassed one now, one who was worried by the examiners' impending visit.

"I've come for my father," he said. And when I told him where his father was he sat down and I brought him coffee. He said, "I *told* him They weren't coming. I told him and told him and you are my witness, Billy; but he would *not* believe me."

Oh I wasn't going to argue with him then and there; neither the time nor the place for it. Besides, I admired the route he had chosen, going his own way, not following, rummaging about with his own hand in the mung of the sub-basement. (Indication of doubt? Yes, perhaps, but I was not aware of it then. Lust of the chase was in me; in the tension of pursuit I examined nothing but merely followed the map, as if it were ancient writ. I had received the call, the sleeping hero had waked and I stumbled after like a starving peasant, a dislocated weaver longing for the manor, frightened in the walled city. We'll never make that mistake again, will we, friend?)

"I have to go after him, Billy, and get him back." He placed the cup so carefully in the saucer, as if he were setting up a monument to himself. "I must get him back, Bill. I need him. He is full of secrets and I must keep him till he dies. He'll tell all on his deathbed, Billy. I know it, I know he will."

I offered to take him with me, as far as the rendezvous point. Well, why not? It was nothing to me. My heart beat to another rhythm. I had the hardness, the detachment only the truly committed can know. A rented uniform a day ago, now it was mine. Not easy; it's not easy to grow a new skin, but I have it now and am easy in it. My mission had settled about my shoulders. I had made the grand repudiation, was giving up the world and all.

Through the window I could see Reverend Flowers, followed by those who remained, walking toward the grotto for sunrise services; there they would wait for news of triumph. Gunner was on his knees at the entrance. It was time. It was time. I drank the last of the coffee and led Greely to my car. In the beginning he had refused but even he now was following the general, no matter that he did so unwillingly or with bad grace. We make our flat refusals, dear, don't we?—and then find ourselves doing their will anyway. How does it come about? We are all so tied together, watcher and watched, enemy and enemy, that even *No* becomes an affirmation, because it can be used. (And if you don't believe me, friend, watch them dickering at Geneva, preparing their disasters and speaking of *tragic choice*. Never mind; we shall rout them yet and save this sweet apple, the last best hope of man.)

Stepping into the Plymouth was like coming home. Long time, I said and patted the wheel; drove across the camp and onto the highway where a film of sand shifted like taffeta under the wheels. The desert barely tolerated the highway; if we turned our backs, sand and wind would make short work of it. Table land; as we approached the Beauty Ranch it seemed to rise up out of the flat earth, as Chartres did when last I was in uniform.

Passing it, I said farewell to Beatrice. Farewell, Beatrice, it's too late now, it's too late for you; the pre-Asian pox will be on you forever, nasty as superfluous hair, underarm odor, unsightly bulge.

Greely was silent. I said, "I'll leave the keys; you can have my car. You'll need it for getting back."

He looked at me, then shook his head. "They're not coming, Bill," he said. (Oh the irony of it, eh, friend? That he who denied and denied it should now be living in the heavenly place and walking freely about that great plaza; robe and staff, in beauty forever.) "I have a loyalty to my science," he said, as explanation for not taking my way.

"Mutiny! Exchange loyalties, Junior, and come with us. Mutiny and die so that you may live again and save the world. Listen, Junior, I'm going but I am not leaving, understand that. I'll be back, and soon, with a packful of knowledge, all the secrets you've been seeking. My resurrection will take place *here,* make no mistake about that! I would not be going if I thought otherwise, Junior."

Impossible to convince him; he maintained a spoiled boy's silence. But it seemed right to have him with me. I thought of his wife. Doris. Then immediately put such thoughts from my mind. Not difficult, for soon we came to the abandoned mine and as we approached the door of the shack burst open and a woman, platinum-blonde hair blinking like a beacon as she turned, stumbled out, fetters still trailing from her left wrist. I increased speed and drove past; could not stop for her; that would have spoiled everything.

"What was that? Who was she?" Junior asked.

"Must be the prospector's wife."

"Dressed like that?"

She was wearing a filmy lilac evening gown. I said nothing. That mere glimpse of her (the hair) was enough to tell me they had kidnaped the wrong woman. I had been opposed to it in the first place. Their silly publicity schemes could debase our mission in the minds of some; but we are all captives of our time, even us, the chosen who have not yet been purged. I looked in the rear-view mirror and saw her walking back toward the Beauty Ranch, her skirt held up above her ankles, revealing silver shoes.

Now I made the turn-off, onto the secondary road; and forty minutes later I pulled up beside the empty command car and the truck. We got out and walked to the edge of the butte: deep steps spread to the desert floor, five hundred feet below. Greely cried, "Father! Father!" and began the descent, jumping from step to step. Those below did not look up; the general signaled me, acknowledging my presence, then looked at his watch. The Indians unloaded the dynamite; the smudge pots had already been set out in a wide circle, their oily smoke to serve as signal for the craft, a way of marking the spot. As if They needed such aids! But the general must do things the way they've always been done; real change comes and he moves forward in the same old shoes. Too bad, but we've got to make do with those we have; leaders always have mean qualities, or nearly always. When the Day comes I will show myself liberated from human flaws, having been taught perfection. Standing there I had a vision of my shining forehead; and my eyes filled with tears, so keen was my longing.

Greystone's voice rose to the top of the butte, bounced up every step, overtook Greely who was halfway down; the Indians, responding, moved more quickly. I counted the cases of dynamite stacked against the powerhouse: seven, and they were bringing up more! How stupid, oh how stupid are the very old and the very tired and the very desperate; take it as a rule of thumb, friend: those lacking in energy lack also cunning. I could hear Ironsides' fusty voice saying, "Well, general, we have ten boxes—why not use ten boxes?" And Greely, Sr., or young Heffernan or one of the others I saw now—top of heads and tips of shoes, cartoons of men—saying, "Let's give 'em a real big bang. Let's let 'em hear us!" I needn't tell you, friend: with us Americans, life's a picnic to the very end.

A wind sprang up then—I took it as sign of Their imminent arrival—and curled the sand around the powerhouse, started eddies all the way to the horizon; I heard its whisper behind me and saw the sand form perfectly engineered drifts against the hubcaps of my Plymouth.

The dynamite was set; Greystone paid out the wire; I could see the crimping tool in his hand. Two Indians squatted by the charge-box, the plunger black against the sun-bright sand. Surely they'd move back, surely they'd move back! I said, aghast, for they were too close. Bad enough if they had used half the charge, the five boxes I had ordered; but suicide this way. Greystone surely would see that; he'd order them back. He knelt and joined the wire. The Indians had saddled up again; they cantered in tight circles in the blowing sand and I could hear their warbling, triumphant chant. The general stood (too close! too close!) with his legs apart, hands on hips: oh that classic stance! would they never learn! The others clustered behind him. Greystone raised his hand and looked to the general for the signal. I shouted but they did not hear. Was there danger? I asked myself. Could I properly judge distance from this height, from this peculiar perspective? So my mind worked, urging surrender, making cowardice possible; but my body, better self, had started out; I leapt from terraced edge to edge, saw Greely, Jr., arrive at the bottom and run to where his father stood with the others; but did not see the signal given. Judah's roar; the concussion was like a gigantic hiccup that stopped the natural order of things: air, sound, light, all. Dazed, unsocketed, I saw a horse on its side, kicking, scraping a place for itself in the desert floor.

thirty-four

GONE. I WOKE thinking *Gone,* it is gone, that concrete fort and its programmed heart pulsing with messages and alarms; become debris, handfuls of pebbles like shrapnel low in the sky when the lion's roar was finally heard there at the desert's center. A great unfolding. Extrapolation of dreams. The butte melted like butter and my Plymouth's front wheels heaved at the new edge made by sound's power; like a newly created animal my car was, its chrome snout chomping at the butte's tender lip, eating its support away. Got a brain the size of a pea, I thought; and I counted it as lost. Oh yes, I still had my wits about me.

The sand coiled up in ropy spouts, joined at last to become a gigantic winding sheet that soon enshrouded all. Groping my way in this cloud I grasped the mane of a riderless horse that plunged, wild-eyed, at my shoulder; but he calmed to my touch, scenting the odor of my urgency. I mounted, my knee knocking against the long leather rifle-holster, and I rode in circles, circling the smudge pots, hallooing for a landing. No dice. Only the moon responded; then, the sun. (Rumors of me are, I think, getting about in this land, *even* in this land of distances.)

In the deaf, terrible tides I ran, peninsulas of light across my portholes. I gentled my mount; my wrists were cunning and I nudged him forward, toward the breakers, with my knees. I saw certain things, advancing toward the desert's secret heart, delicious tightly wound red flower; sighted incredible Floridas. Never mind; memory must not be forced and it won't do to turn to another for aid. It's enough, I think, to say I knew the languor of the lost. When the time comes for the writing of the third testament these notes will be useful. I am making a record. It will have to be consulted. To be hero and Thucydides both is no small thing, friend, but I have done it. Name another if you can.

Woke thinking *Gone;* and the man wearing the leather mask bent over me and said, "At last, white man;

you've been out like a light for two days and two nights."

I was lying on a cornhusk mattress that rustled when I moved. The woman in the corner bent to her loom, comb snuffled among the threads and the wood treadle lunged toward an end I could not understand. Outside the open door children jumped rope and chanted rhymes. Adobe walls. The Indian wet my lips with water from a gourd. So fitting, I thought; and slept again; and did not even know what day it was until I bought a newspaper in Phoenix. (I left them my horse, cashed a traveler's check at the trading post and caught the bus to the city. No one questioned me.)

I bought back issues of the local papers and a plane ride home to Pittsburgh. No one tried to stop me. I studied the papers. I read every line. Blackout almost total, a one-day wonder: powerhouse destroyed, three Indians captured by the Arizona National Guard. But you know all that, friend, you read it yourself; millions did, and never paused to think of its meaning but turned to the sports and the daily torpor of life as we live it now.

thirty-five

WE'RE ALMOST finished. The last Days are upon us; soon we can draw the double line at the bottom of the page and leave it for those others who will gather to make the concordance and write The Commentaries, who will seek in every word the image of the loving shepherd. Meanwhile, there is a marked rise in the urgency of things and I shall soon step forward to announce myself. Rumors of me are getting about.

Only some few items remain to be noted for the record, and a few questions asked.

Is the general dead? What of the Greelys, father and son? Have they been put away in that place in Alaska? Or did they make the planned getaway and are they now in the home place? Newspapers of course have revealed nothing; the news is managed, controlled by Intelligence; but from other sources reports come in of sightings: much activity in the Twelvepalms area.

Reports of a great mother-ship hovering over the desert with three small ships for escort; they were launched from her back and scouted low over the desert floor, apparently looking for something. People living in a village near the desert's rim heard at dawn a sound in the sky: it was like an organ, one note, held for five minutes or more, said the local police chief. During that night other residents were wakened by a knocking at their doors. We have had messages from our people in that area: descriptions of a great luminosity in the northern skies, of curious localized turbulence in the air, erratic migrations of birds; of enormous clouds appearing suddenly in a cloudless sky, clouds the wind did not move. (The ships often use this method to screen themselves from our eyes.) Also, unelaborated newspaper accounts of strange occurrences at the Indian reservation: a prayer dance was performed for the first time in living memory—preparation for the end of the world, the Indians said. Other tribes came from great distances. Rumors spread worldwide of a storm that would destroy the earth: prayer meetings attended by tens of thousands in India; in Saigon a Buddhist priest burned himself to death, a sacrifice to the great power.

Did they then, that handful of men, make the definitive escape from the watchers and the pursuers? All the evidence points to it.

The old men in the garage, sensing in the air the strange turbulence, are in a state of great excitement; they stay late every night, until dawn, waiting, certain they are next, that Junior's coming back for them. They're packed and ready.

I have taken up Greely's work. I waited two months and when I knew the time was right I packed my bags, crated my books, and took Junior's place. Now it is I who stand at the machine and strike a note from the violin and watch the numbers rise in the ledger of experiments. Doris continues the lectures, the old men make their weekly contributions, more open-handed now than ever; and every night I lie beside her, in her soft maternal embrace. She does not look directly at my face. I know that she, preacher's daughter, feels my radiance.

Some nights the power in me nibbles at my fingertips,

demanding release, and I get up and hurry to the work, set the molecules to dance and strain against the force that binds them. And I strain and push myself, urged on by the sound of the hoofs of those wild horses. I hear them always at my back, rushing headlong toward the ultimate madness. Oh but I've got this thing between my teeth, friend, I've got the bit now and I'll run with it, hair flowing in a wind of my own making. I'll head them off, the maddened beasts, before they reach the terrible abyss, flanks heaving, nostrils distended, wild-eyed; at the last moment, friend, in the classical Western tradition I'll save (I will!) this apple world, this sweet nut, this beauty, beauty. Ah listen, hear the bugle blow, the pennant snap in the crystal wind? Beleaguered pioneers, hold out! Only hold out!